Video Store

By Matt Madigan

For Mike and Andrea

Forever video love

IN MEMORIUM

Clarence Reid

And all these faggots would be walking right by and I'd be laughing my ass off at them scurrying along to make the starting bell. Not at the desk on time? Get ready for your boss to drag you in front of the whole crew and go right up inside your can; soon people start to like it. Sure I limp, but you know what, I've got a nice house and a VCR. And when that machine inevitably becomes all important to them, I slide in as the pusher. I'm behind the register smiling away at the steady stream of junkies all trying to get out of their heads and slide into somewhere else. And all of them were so ready to give me their cash.

Almost everyone who was kept downtown had to walk past my place sometime during their day. The perfect location: right on the corner, across from a huge parking lot for two large apartment buildings and a big ass banking building. To our right was a gourmet pizza place we never ate at, but man it drew the people to us on a Friday night for a post-Cosby entertainment fix. People who knew I was the owner treated me like somebody. It was the life, but when people told me how lucky I was, that would drive me out of my fucking mind.

Those people weren't doing the Ramen Noodle diet for over a year, shoving any cent of profit back into the place. Scraping to find more tapes and grow the library. With my eye for great film, and Evan's keen insight into what movie philistines want, plus the fact that it was here or rent your tapes out of some creepy guy's gasoline-smelling shed where he's got about twenty cum stained third generation bullshit vids, this place could not lose. We became the only show in town.

Our competition really was a few of those nasty cellar places, and one guy who would rent tapes out of his

1977 banged up gray and white murder van. One time he smashed our front window. He was such a lard ass though, and it took him a lot longer than he figured to run back across the street after the tedious task of throwing a brick into a window three feet in front of him. Evan saw the whole thing. I called the fucker later that night and told him we would take his entire stock as compensation, or we could call the cops. He blanched at first, but then remembering he was on probation for a hit and run, he agreed. Crushing him, and adding his collection of mostly good-plus dupes, brought in the real film fans. These were my people and I looked forward every day to talking with them. Most died a little during the day in an office or somewhere, but lived at night with help from the pusher.

We had become the center of something, and almost nothing could have been more exciting. And if the store slowed down during the day, we'd take out our *Dark Tower* and play a couple of games. I was two thirds of the way to having everything that I could ever want. Everything I did was the right thing. Never before had I ever felt that anything I did was even remotely correct. But I forced change, and everything was expanding in front of me. What Metropolitan Video meant was that I had clawed to the top and become a free man.

Turn it on Again by Genesis is playing out into the store from Evan's boom box that pretty much stays here now. I'm making sure all our cases are where they should be. The four copies of *Howard the Duck* on the shelves for a dollar each is the reason Evan is not allowed to call in tape orders anymore. Carrie is sitting in the back room wearing her uniform. She could have been a porn star if her face wasn't that same as her cousin's, and that guy looks just like George Gobel, glasses and all. The two live together in Evan's dad's Mc-mansion. His old man is filthy with money, and the place is so big that half the clan moved in with them after some shit happened.

She takes out my mix, and puts in the *Material Girl* ca-single. Right before I can tell her to knock off the shit, she starts shaking what momma gave her all over the place. And then it starts crawling through me; slowly at first, but I can't fight it. You've been there too. Just something flares up way down in there and you're left no fucking choice. I turned on my heel and ran to the bathroom; used some shampoo this time and shower babies hit in the bowl in a genocidal rain. My teeth hurt for a few minutes from grinding down. I washed up without looking at myself in the mirror over the sink.

In the back room, I slide a tape of *Unknown Pleasures* into our old stereo to drown out that shit she's still playing. Stuff sticks in my head too easily, and one time it was *Holiday in Cambodia*, and that was one long fucking month. Standing on one of the chairs I push the smoke-stained ceiling tile up, and take down our community bag and pipe. Pull out a Coke from this fridge we found in an alley behind here the day we moved in. Half way through *Disorder* I am all set up and Carrie comes in, lights up a cigarette and sits on the futon.

"Just don't blow it at me, okay?"

"Why?"

"I don't want to smell like that. It's gross."

"I am king here you know?"

"Co-king."

"Shut up."

And here comes Evan, sporting pleated white pants, and this button up shirt which is not only striped red and blue, but has four big white pockets with horizontal zippers over the front. The wide open white collar really does the trick. The hard-as-a-brick-of-frozen-shit feathered hair on top on the whole deal just seals the flavor right in. If he were not an independent business man, surely he could get a job, probably part time, standing in the window of almost any Chess King throughout the area. Get ready to duck some serious Oran Julius cups.

Carrie drops her butt into a quarter full can of RC, and swishes the thing around. How Evan drinks that shit is beyond me. She gets up, tells us to stay sober and make some money, then heads off for her job. We nuke up some pizzas and we dig in at the bell. Then we get into some Hot Pockets. After that, just to settle down out guts, we have a smoke. It is pretty much every day; Fucking Heaven on Earth.

Certain people come in here on the same day, and rent the same movies over and over. It would cost so much less to buy it, but every Thursday afternoon this guy from the doctor's building down the street comes in and rents *Romancing the Stone*. I even offered to sell him a used copy, but he said no. In fact, he told me he'd never gotten around to watching it, and he keeps renting in hopes of having some free time soon. Even so, I said, why not buy it? No. He'd rather rent. I don't care, he makes me money. I started checking the tapes when he'd return them, because we *always* rewind them, and he's one of those types who would rather pay a dollar than do it. Last year he paid $48 alone in rewind fees. He *was* watching the tape probably every time he rented it, because the thing was always in the same place. After trying hard not to look for the longest time, I gave in and checked out what scene he must be watching. Sometimes I should look away, but I never do. It was always stopped right after the scene where Michael Douglas goes head first between Kathleen Turner's thighs.

Most of the business men from the office buildings around here come in with head down, aiming straight for the double saloon doors and right to the porn. You *must* have those type of doors, because people *will* try to jerk off in there. Sometimes even the double doors don't stop them. We make more than half our money on the jerk stuff. We can't get the Ginger Lynn and Traci Lords movies on the shelf fast enough in this place. The only one who can compete with them is Joy Bliss. And the same deal happens with the skin flicks: people renting the same films all the time for one scene or another. Good thing they don't know how to bootleg, which only takes a few cables, a blank tape and two VCRS. But who the hell wants to drop a grand on VCRs except someone like me who is a professional?

The one and only thing I don't like about the place is talking to film philistines who rent the worst movies you can ever imagine. *Back to the Future, Crocodile Dundee, Rocky IV, Cocoon, Fletch,* and even the fucking *Goonies,* a movie which is painfully, mind-numbingly bad. I offer these people alternatives like *Brazil* –Pure brilliance. Jesus even if you must have Hollywood how about *The Color Purple,* but fucking *Goonies?* You're an adult. And these people, they stand there and grin away, so excited to go home and watch this tripe. That is why Carrie is so perfect in this place when she helps out, because not only do guys dig her, there is not a film on the planet she does not like. No matter what anyone puts on the counter in front of her, she thinks it's great. I will do anything to not talk about film with her. And Evan is only slightly better. But they know what the commoners like, so I take their advice when buying some of our stock.

There are, though, two parts of the store which are *strictly* mine. The cult and horror sections are a true fan's wet dream. I have five John Waters films: *Polyester, Female Trouble, Eat Your Makeup/Mondo Trasho* (bootleg), and even *Pink Flamingos. I've got Faces of Death, Mondo Cane* and *Mondo Cane II, Videodrome, Scanners, Night of the Living Dead, Dawn of the Dead,* and *Zombi!* There are copies (*plural*) of *Eraserhead,* (possibly the only ones in the Commonwealth), and a decent copy of Passolini's *Salo: 120 Days of Sodom.* I even have some screeners. A lot aren't first generation, you just can't get these classics, but my stuff is as clean as the source will allow. Just look at the racks: *Cruising, Emmanuelle in America,* (un-fucking-cut with the fake snuff and the horse scene), *Killer Nun, Corrupt* with Spanish subtitles and starring Johnny Rotten, *Rolling Thunder, Voodoo Black Exorcist, Brazil, The Projectionist* with a youngish Rodney Dangerfield, *Black Belt Jones* with Jim Kelly, *Chained Heat, Born to Kill, The Mack, Truck Turner, Ministry of Fear,* on and on. Some were recorded off TV, but they still all look great. Up to date runs of *Manimal, Automan, The Phoenix, Street Hawk,* even *Sanford and Son,* and *All in the Family.* I taped and cut the commercials off re-runs. It is just like with drugs, no one gives a rat's ass where it comes from, as long as it gets them high.

Sometimes I'll allow a real film freak to take something out for free in exchange for letting me boot what they have. Got a lot of cool *Doctor Who* episodes that way. People in New Hampshire get it on PBS channel 11, but I don't because I have cable. I also am making cash taping and renting *The Cosby Show, Cheers*, and anything else customers who can't figure out how to push the record button. Several of the police have me record *Hill Street Blues* for the station house. For the firemen, it is old episodes of *Adam 12*.

The only problem I've ever had here was with this one chick what got all haughty with me saying *Suspiria* was superior to *Carnival of Souls*. Called bullshit quick on that one. It got so heated she swore never to come back until I admitted I was wrong. Might have praised that movie, but the way she went off on Not in my place sister. But for all that noise, I got some great people like the famous DJ Jazz who takes to the airwaves alongside his Mistress of the Night, Lady M, "long after decent people are asleep." The guy is a huge fan of the show *The Phoenix*. We have watched the thing up and down in the backroom, picking out any clues we can.

Evan and I also hang out in the back before and after hours, maybe play some D&D, or watch films on the TVs above the front counter. In the back is our sanctuary. Many late-night discussions have gone on there between him and me and the bong, about what the fuck it is all about. I am digging it here so much that I often sleep on the futon, which is pretty crappy, but I don't care. Other nights I'll end up back at my place, which is an in-law apartment over my dad's detached two car garage. Suits me perfectly. There is a stairway on the side with a private entrance. It is nice and quiet and has everything I'll ever need: a bed, my chair, TV and VCR, Kitchenette with a microwave, dorm fridge and half stove. Dad only charges me $25 a week, which is nothing to me.

I've got quite the esoteric collection of film ephemera stored here. Over the years I've written to studios and cultivated relationships with people. They talk to me because I don't want to be a star. What I want is original stuff from sets, but nothing too big. I have a Styrofoam coffee cup Darren McGavin drank out of on the set of *The Night Stalker*, a cigarette butt each from Debbie Harry and James Woods from *Videodrome*-had to work a connect in Canada for those. Dude had a job on the set cleaning up, and snagged all sorts of shit like that. Traded him a complete set of the first three months of *Dark Shadows* Barnabas Collins story line for pretty much a couple of filters. I have about a dozen cigarettes smoked by celebs in my place. They all smell and taste differently.

All the framed posters on the walls and ceiling are originals: *Bladerunner, Shivers* and *Videodrome,* are pristine, as is almost everything else here. The window in the bathroom aims into the backyard where I can blow all the smoke I want, and the old man is none the wiser. Most of my personal video collection I keep beneath my bed, secured in three large plastic tubs. Copies of many of these tapes reside at the store now; their pristine masters are kept here.

It is the last day of September, and we are coming down from a full moon, when we finally get in these two new Olympus VHS Camcorders. The plan is to rent these suckers out for twenty-five bucks a day, with a fifty-dollar deposit on your credit card. These fuckers cost, but I'm feeling people will rent the things like crazy. Imagine you can record your kid's birthday party and watch it right after it happens–almost *as* it happens. Capturing time. And we gave you the tape for free; cost to us about three dollars. By that Friday we had a waiting list of twenty people. This is the sign that we have been waiting for, screaming "here comes the cash!" Come spring and summer everyone will want these things for graduations, weddings, all that happy horseshit. Then we might just open our own bank.

As soon as a camera is returned, one of us is on the phone to the next person on the waiting list, and they fly right down here. Everyone was really cool about bringing the things back on time, even though they can't seem to remember their late videos at the same time. It only takes a week before one dickhead forgets about it. A guy named Robert Samuel, and here we really go. I leave a call on his machine and within an hour this barrel-chested cocky gorilla comes hotfooting in, drops the camera case on the counter and heads out.

"Excuse me sir," I say. "There is a late fee on this."

"Just charge it to my card," going out the door without looking back.

Evan runs his card number off the mimeograph sheet in his file. I bring the camera to the backroom and check it all out. Everything is there, including the videotape.

"Hey homo, can you still see that guy who dropped off the camera?"

"He's gone. Good thing too, he was double parked."

"Double parking dickhead, one of those huh? I ain't callin' him," taking his tape and dropping it into a highly unstable pile of stuff on our card table. It was just one thing too many and down it all slides: unmarked tapes, *Fangoria* magazines, old issues of *Creepy* or *Eerie*, (there's really no difference), pizza boxes once configured together like the TARDIS, dozen or so two liters of Jolt and Mountain Dew, a dupe of *Closer* I made for Evan which he never listened to, and a bunch of papers and stuff. All it slowly dumps into the corner, and now the table is clean again.

The next guy on the camcorder list is this steroid creep who doesn't want anyone to know, yet everyone knows, that he is aka a stripper and sometimes gigolo named Dick James. A few years ago, he was combing the beaches and high school football games, telling teenage girls he was a camera man from MTV scouting for models. When I was there, he was around trying to run this pussy scam with a Polaroid instamatic saying he was from a modelling magazine. Because he is so utterly stupid, he gets sniffed out quickly, and then gets shoved into the oven hat and all. And so, he bides his time and the kids get older and the new parents have never heard of him. Now he has returned and is ready for new ghosts to capture on tape. He never touches these girls as far as I've heard. He just wants the images; safer that way for everyone. Still a creep though. Still take his money though.

Today I am wearing a gray t-shirt with a bold red MAD logo screaming along the neckline, with the words beneath: Mutually Assured Destruction/YES ME WORRY! I made the thing myself from a t-shirt kit I got about a year ago at the mall. This was my first one, and it came out decent. I came up with the idea after an intense *Gamma World* sessiom with Evan and our gaming buddy Lenny. I think the idea is actually comforting: Everyone dead. No suffering. Begin again. And that is where our campaign began, right after the end. It lasted a good few months, but it became depressing even for me to see two groups killing one another over a can opener.

That very day of the first night of it all, we were continuing our three-year D&D campaign. I was running and the other two played two characters each. Evan was of course a hack and slash fighter, but also a Gnome Illusionist/Thief named Skall that I thought was his best character. He always did a good job of playing him; anytime he would stroke his big schnozzle, he was getting into Skall mode. Lenny played two twins, one a Magic User and the other a Cleric. Everyone was around seventh or eighth level, and we were playing the really overdone but fantastically fun *S2: Expedition to the White Plume Mountains.* The last session stopped right before the players were about to meet one very nasty vampire. I wanted to have a night game, but Evan said he had somewhere to go, and Lenny had to "get home." Then he splashed some Brut Faberge over his face and neck, took his prisoner's outfit from hanging in the bathroom, removed his blue weed stinking Roo sweat suit he keeps here, and put his uniform back on.

The wind was blowing like crazy that night, so I decide to camp out right in the back with some Hot Pockets, a six pack of Coke, a full pipe and a brilliantly clear copy of *Blood Sucking Freaks*. It was as comfortable to me as the coziest den in all Victorian London. I just about made it to the end of that pure classic before sleep showed up and the winds got sick of blowing. Not sure how long I was out, but this noise is in my dream before I realize that it's coming from the waked-up world. I sit up in the futon and someone is trying to pry their way into the store through the back door. I flick on the floor lamp next to me and see the turn lock is already undone. The door is metal and we always keep a wooden bar across the thing after closing, which is the only thing stopping this crazy fucker.

"Get outta here, I've got a gun!" voice high and thin. My heart pounding and pounding and pounding and I am trying not to puke. Then whoever it is starts kicking the door. I grab the cordless phone, pull the antenna up and call the cops, fumbling around in the toolbox next to the fridge the whole time.

The reinforcement is holding up, but the edges of the frame are pulling away from the jamb.

"I just called the cops, and *I've got a gun!*"

This big hairy gorilla man-arm reaches through an opening on the side and starts fumbling around for the bar. I run up and drive a Phillips head screwdriver into the meat between his left thumb and forefinger. He pulls back right quick with a ripping snort, the screwdriver popping out. The ogre falls back, tearing into some crazy language. He starts kicking away, but sirens and lights are entering the scene now and he books down the alley. I just stand there panting, staring at the screwdriver with this little bit of blood on the tip, until the cops start banging on the front door. I kick the thing under the futon along with my weed gear, then run out front to let them in. There are two of them, one splitting around to the back, but I know the guy is gone. The other one, who is a real hard looking chick came back inside with me.

She goes: "Smells like you were having a good time."

Without missing a beat, except in my chest, I point to the door and tell her what went down, sans the stabbing. Then the thing fell in with her partner standing in the opening, looking down at it.

"Well," he said, "it was literally one *tap* away from falling over. You got lucky."

"What is with the blood on the floor?" she says to me.

"He cut his hand somehow, trying to break in. I saw it when he reached in. You could take a sample."

"Makes sense. But we're not going to take a sample. Probably just a druggie."

We all go out in front and I give them a statement. The chick won't let it go that perhaps I had smoked pot or even still had some. She starts into me until the other one butts in.

"We're not here for that," he says. "We will file this report. Probably just some junkie or something. Lot of drugs gets sold near the banks. Weird, huh?"

"Yeah."

The chick goes: "Okay young man, clean up your act."

I say nothing.

The two get into their cruiser and ride down the street, fading to black. I run right into the back and prop the door up as best I can, pushing some of the screws back in and that's enough to slide the wooden bar through its brackets and keep it in place for now. I get a hammer and do the best I can. I push the futon and filing cabinet up against it. I want to call Evan, or someone, but it is really late or really early, so I just pace around the place for a while. After a while a cruiser passes by with its search light on the sidewalk; most likely closing out the investigation. A lot of cold air is blasting in from the sides and beneath the door, making it shake every so often and always scaring the shit out of me. I put a claw hammer on my lap, wrapped myself with an old 1977 Star Wars blanket and stared at that fucking door until it was one big blur.

Evan found me sitting right there, eyes empty, bags forming. I let him know what had happened, and he holy shitted me about twenty times. Then he called this carpenter that did all the work on this place before we opened. We ordered a stronger door with a metal bar and reinforced braces. I took a mad piss, then drove straight home in my Corolla and went right to bed. My mind was racing, and as I stared up at my *Videodrome* poster of Debbie Harry's mouth, the break-in ran through my mind over and over and over and over, and Jesus fucking Christ no matter what I did that reel would not stop looping on my screen. I had a smoke in the bathroom, which didn't do much to calm me down, but my mind was open and the screen was about a 14 incher with two speakers, creating fake stereo, and it is time for my favorite show LIFE WITH HENRY. The only one the Cosby Show trails in ratings. And the music is out of my control sadly, and it is some synth-pop bullshit nowhere like New Order but much more like Thompson Twins in an optimistic key.

There's the house 1428 North Genesee Ave. White with no fence, but an immaculate lawn, three windows on each side of the red door. Above are three windows on each side. The roof is green and there are tall, well-manicured trees popping out from the perfect back yard over the top of the house. And she comes through the front door with a smile so pleasant you can't believe it. It's one of those real generic housewives; someone sort of like Stephanie Zimbalist. Not a lot of variation here, but that is what the people like. In fact, the actresses are triplets. They interchange to avoid union rules and when I am sick of one, I just swap them out. I only really know them by how deep they can take me down.

Then we pan around and here is our nutty friend Hank played by some Scott Baio/Willie Aimes level talent. He comes over sometimes when our one black character Tyrone, a requisite in these shows, visits us. Who can forget the time Hank splashed ink all over his face by accident and Tyrone thought it was his long-lost cousin? Or the time we had the dinner party and no one could figure out who was the butler and who was the guest because an exhaust pipe had blown all over my moon-white face. It really was a scream for all of us. And of course my wife and I have a cutest as buttons little kid we adopted named Kim, and he is a math genius from China. A baby we saved from Communism. Actually, he's is three Asian babies from the same family that we all pay out of petty cash.

As the music fades, a few commercials play by my eyes, and then we are in the kitchen, a set certainly, a studio audience full of people off the street who have nothing better to do than go to tapings in the middle of the day. We pump fresh oxygen in and give them cold wine in Styrofoam cups or warm cannabis cookies to make things more pleasant for everyone. And then there is the star. I got this show coming off my stand-up tour where I told everyone to fuck off. The station loved my audacity and after murdering the censors, I was still unable to gain entrance into the control room; I still must play by some rules here for some reason. Why? Isn't it my screen?

The wind rattling the big leafless tree out front woke me up around six. I showered and changed into an Iggy Pop t-shirt and black jeans, then headed back to my store. The lights were orangey downtown. Maybe the city changed them for the holiday season. Paper skeletons and horror masks were popping up in dimly lit windows. My place was hopping when I got there. At eight we ordered some pizzas and ate in shifts in the back. I was fucking famished and went at it like the Wolfman on a sheep's carcass. Usually I love eating, but not that night. That night it was for sheer survival. Around nine only the real movie fans were around. I spent time near my sections, talking to a few regulars about *The Holy Mountain,* and what Jodorowsky's vision of *Dune* would have been like. One guy even said he liked the Lynch version. I shut him down with a quick, "No Geiger, no Dune!" Everyone agreed.

Once I check those guys out, I lock up and walk into the back. Evan and Carrie are there smoking cigarettes and drinking wine coolers. She's wearing black stretch pants, white leg warmers over them and a white "Frankie Says Relax." He's right out of some Chess King catalog, with the Z-Cavarichi jeans and the big hair and opened shirt, and gold chain–the Star of David hanging off it which is solid gold, and as powerful as a cross to a vampire with some of these snobby Yuppie broads who come in here. He's pale as the moon, plus he's got his completely bald ass chest sticking right out for the ladies to admire. He's a great guy, but man does he have the wrong look.

"You missed quite a scene."

"When?"

"When you went home to crash," Evan said opening another bottle.

"What happened?"

"I'm back here with the two guys who are fixing the door when all of a sudden another guy, this big guy right, just walks into the back here and demands to speak to the owner. So I'm thinking, o shit someone's been recording porn over the kids' tapes again, and this guy's kid saw people bumping uglies."

"O shit."

"Well after I calmed the guy down a bit. And he's this big guy who's blowing his stack. But you know I used the old Jewish persuasion, and calmed him down. And I was really baked. So anyways the guy said he put a home tape into the wrong box and needed it back. He can't remember what box it was in and on and on. So then he goes 'I'm a lawyer,' and the tape is a deposition he desperately needs. I told him I didn't have anything like that. Then he tells me I'd better have it to him by tomorrow or we," his thumb going between him and me, "could both go to jail."

"You cannot go to jail for that. Guys, c'mon," says Carrie.

"You call the cops?"

"Yeah and I filed a report, like we always do."

"What did they say?"

"*Nothing*. They were probably pissed off they had to come back here."

"Did you call any of your seventeen lawyer relatives?"

"No need. I have them all on retainer."

"*Wait*," it broke into my head as I said that. "Shit, was his hand bandaged?"

"He had leather gloves on."

"Even inside?"

"Yeah. So what?"

"Remember I stabbed the guy in the hand?"

"I didn't know you stabbed him," Carrie said looking up, sort of impressed. "I can also ask around and see if there was anyone in the ER last night who was stabbed in the hand."

"By a screwdriver."

"A stabbing is a stabbing. We would still have to report it. Wow. This is just like Encyclopedia Brown mysteries. Remember those?"

"'Cept there's no back of the book to turn to. I mean what could be on that tape?"

Then I get this weird, metallic taste in my mouth: "Holy shit, I just remembered some guy left a tape in a camcorder a few days ago. It was the guy before Dick James."

Evan gets up and goes through the rental slips in our three-drawer filing cabinet. He starts waving it around like it is some living creature fighting against him; one of those flying things in *It Conquered the World*. Sadly, he isn't doing a bit.

"Robert Samuel," he says, letting it flutter in front of his face.

"Yeah, I remember the name. It must've been his tape. Must be something really good on it."

"Well, where is it?" says Carrie.

"I don't know. I'll have to dig around. You know everything is everywhere here somewhere."

"He did leave an address on the rental sheet."

I stood up and took the phone book out from under the front counter. There is no lawyer under that address or even name. I look at the front of the book, and there is no such person listed in town.

"That's weird man."

Then I knew they had to go. My heart was racing and I wanted to puke. They just needed to leave, and leave now. I sort of talked around it, and got them out of there as fast as I could. I didn't know why I wanted them out of there, but I had to be alone. It took about twenty minutes, but they went spare and I started rummaging. Found two tapes that might be the. I knew which tape it was right away just by feel; the goddamn thing radiated cold. What the hell could be so important on it? Maybe it was a deposition, and maybe about something really hot.

A behind the scenes bootleg tape on a hot trial or crime could bring in huge cash. I drove home, stopping for some McDonalds on the way, and parked in front of my apartment. I dropped down six cheese burgers and a large fry. I took my Coke and went upstairs to clean my head. Then I fed that fucking thing into the VCR.

It was no doubt the man who rented the camera, buck-ass naked and adjusting the focus. His discolored, gray tight skin over this hard gut; stretch marks everywhere, expanding ugly brown spots. All that werewolf hair on him. And those forearms, exactly like the ones trying to get into the shop. He backs up and revealing a hotel room, shades drawn, and the door down a small hall. Not much happens, and then from around the corner she appears.

The video skips for a second, or maybe it's my screen. She comes into view with these big shining eyes like a cat through the night; wide and full of light from whatever he's got reflecting off her. She looks like Molly Ringwald and is dressed like Madonna the virgin, with the pearls and all, approaching him in screaming silence. The big blonde hair is no doubt a wig; her eyebrows are black. She stares not at the camera, but at me, locking on, clamping down. Calling. They unlock something so deep inside of me that when it breaks free from The Man in the Planet's control, tears start pouring down my face. Not tears for her, but for me. She is an unholy messenger, whispering secrets of the universe to me on my wavelength alone. But then it changes it again because after she does things to him you wouldn't even want to consider. After the worst of it ends, the real horror begins. He wraps his pig fingers around her throat. She quickly begins convulsing and spitting everywhere. She is kicking so fast, so hard, not so fast, not so hard, now not at all. He approaches the camera like a shark spotting you in the cage; reaching over the camera to hit stop. He clears his throat and a third of a second before it goes to static, I swear she starts to sit up.

Like a virgin

My head feels like it has been split open by a Bohemian Ear Spoon. I sit down at the table in the back room and have two Boston Crèmes with a can of really cold Fanta from the fridge. When I am not drinking it, I keep it pressed to the back of my neck. That does nothing to help, so I lock the door, push up the ceiling panels and retrieve my stash. I do my best to snap my mind into alignment. The pain slows and all ambient sounds are dulled to an acceptable level of annoyance. This doesn't last.

"And you are *sure* you locked the front door *and* set the alarm last night?"

"Positive. You know I am anal about that, and *super* careful after the break-in attempt."

"So the front door was unlocked and the alarm turned off."

"Yup. But I had to make sure you hadn't swung by first and did that for some reason."

"Why would I do it?" starting to walk to the back.

"I had to make sure, faggot."

"You're the faggot."

"And don't worry, I went and made sure everything is still here. Everything was in place, even the thirty bucks we always leave in the register. I don't get it."

"Why don't we take a look at the tape, huh?"

"Now you're talking."

Before hustling them out last night, the three of us decided the best bet was to abandon the store and let whoever was going to break in to do it when we weren't around. This would avoid real danger, but we also weren't going down that easily. I set up a camcorder with an eight hour tape in it, put the thing inside a display for the *Remo Williams* video, cut a hole cut in it atop the partition between the front and back of the store, aimed it at the front door, and hit record. I put a piece of black tape over the red light.

Evan retrieves the tape, and we stick it into our VCR. It isn't twenty minutes after I set the alarm and then lock the door that the porno pig man comes up to the front and examines our lock under his flashlight beam.

Then he pulls out this large ring of keys and opens it up after a few tries.

"Sorry I doubted you, man."

"How the hell did he get a key?"

"I dunno. He's got enough of them there, look."

It enters the store, slinking right into the back room.

"That's him. The dude I stabbed."

At one point off camera we hear him making a phone call. Most of it is too muffled, but we do both pick up, "everything is fine here." For about fifteen minutes you can hear him like a racoon in your garbage. He comes back into shot carrying two tapes. He places them near the door, takes a Polaroid Instamatic from his coat and takes some shots of our counters and shelves.

"What the hell is *this* about?"

"Dunno."

After pocketing the pictures, he snatches the tapes and hurries out the door.

Over the rest of the dozen, we watch the scene play out twice more.

"Should we call the cops?"

"No fucking way."

We watched the rest of the tape on 4x fast forward, and there is nothing else. As we prep the store for opening, you can feel that ghost. Its invisible ectoplasm is everywhere. I can feel it everywhere. Spend this time in my head, trying to figure out how to purify it. Business is steady that morning, and profitable. I still take off for an early lunch and run down to the library. I've seen enough movies to know a thing or two about detective work, especially from *Hardcore* with George C.

Scott and Peter Boyle. It certainly has its flaws, but that "turn it off! Turn it off!" moment is still amazing. Watch Boyle's face and how much he is enjoying it all. Why not, he practices mind sciences. I pull the city directory and look up the address the guy put on the rental slip. The address turns out to be a YMCA in town here. Bullshit. Something will match up here. It takes me a few, and I dig up two. One is a mill worker downtown. The other Robert Samuel lives in an upscale place with his wife Maureen and their two children Jacki and Robert, Jr. He lists his occupation as: Chief of Police.

I can't get back to the store fast enough.

As I come bombing inside Evan is ringing up someone renting a Nintendo NES system. Because we are the place to be, we landed these things as a limited test run. We charge five bucks a day for it, and a fifty-dollar deposit on your credit card. After Evan cashes the guy out, I rush him into the back room.

"That guy is the goddamn *Chief of Police* here."

"*What?* How do you know?"

"I looked him up at the library."

"Holy Shit. Holy Shit. You think he's the pig-man? Wow. Wow. How fitting really."

"I don't know. I'll go back to the library and look up some old newspaper stories about him."

"Why didn't you do it when you were there?"

"I got too excited and didn't think of it."

"What the hell could be on that tape? And why is he saying that he is a lawyer?"

"I am heading back to the library now."

"No time for even a Hot Pocket?"

"When I come back, maybe some Steakums."

Thirty minutes later I am scrubbing the back issues of the local newspapers. A photo of the guy emerges within fifteen minutes, which I photocopy and head to the store. On the way, I stop in the Korean market and buy a frozen package of Steakums. Back at the fort I hand Evan the copies, and put the food into the microwave. Then I collapse onto the futon.

"You ran all the way back? You know you have your BMX behind the filing cabinets over there, right?"

"*Fuck...*"

"Why didn't you drive?"

"No parking there. It sucks. Get me a Miller out of the fridge, huh?"

He obliges me.

The bell rings on the microwave. Evan peels the steak cuts off the white paper and places them onto sub rolls. He then adds some salt, pepper and a lot of Cheese Whiz. He hands me mine and I dig right in.

"Man are these good."

We wolf it down and then go for another round. Tastes just as good the second time. If I go for a third, it will be one too many, and the taste/pleasure ratio will just plummet. After we wipe our mouths on our sleeves Evan rips a huge Fanta burp and says: "What the hell could be on that tape?"

"Give me an hour."

And about an hour later, he's going: "Holy shit. Holy shit! Holy shit! Look what she's doing to him. I mean *look at that*! She's ramming it right up there. Holy shit man! That is wicked gross! That's some serious faggot shit. *Holy fuck*. What a *fucking faggot*! Turn it off man, I know what it's about now. I don't want to watch any of this gaylord shit. Jesus Christ. Turn it off!"

I can only smile while watching his face reflecting off the screen. He stands up and leaves for the front. I pop the tape out of the deck with that sound just blaring over and over in my head like it is a soundtrack to that magnetic atrocity. This version doesn't have the strangling.

Out front:

"No wonder why he wants it back."

"He's married with kids too."

"Jesus, what a faggot. I mean, you see how big that thing was she had on?"

"Who do you think she is?"

"I don't know. Maybe it is some girl he is like blackmailing or something."

"You think?"

"More like the other way around. She was tooling him and then some. He's a goddamn, fuckin' *gay-lord*, you know that? We could *ruin* that guy. But if we just give it back, *man* would he'd be indebted to us. We could have the Chief in our pocket."

"Yeah. I guess so."

"Should we tell him?"

"I dunno. I did stab the guy."

"*He* doesn't know that."

"He knows someone here did."

"True," Evan says. "But I dunno, I think we gotta give that tape to the Chief ASAP, man. He would never want anyone to know he tried to break into here. We've got all the cards. Let's play this sucker right."

"Yeah, you're right. But I don't want to call him from here. I'm going down the street and use the payphone."

"Good idea."

I scoop a few dimes out of the register and drop them in my pocket. Evan wraps the tape in one of our bags, then places that inside another one. This is the very *Necronomicon* of the video world, and even he knows it. It brims with magic, which only I can control. Head out and start trucking down the street as happy as Mister Natural. At this point I still have every intention in my mind of giving the tape back with no questions asked. The Chief of Police in my back-pocket equals impunity to smoke all the weed I want to and not have to worry about anything. Some guy is acting up at the store, one call and the cops are right there. We could pretty much do anything within a certain reason, just because we did this one solid thing and shut our mouths. But as I pass the S&L building, my face reflecting on its shiny marble, a new option came to me, and the smile melted into the stone. I wasn't sure why I wanted to do it, but everything inside me told me this was the right path to go down. During that three, four-minute walk, something inside me shifted. I still don't know what it was, but my mind just went a different way.

Now I am at the phone on the corner of the street in front of the bank, my hands are trembling and sweat is rolling down my face steady-stream despite the cold wind in my face. I drop in three dimes, hoping my nerve will catch. Twice I hang up before the ringing even begins. But I know it is now or nothing, because there is no way I can do this face to face. I finally connect with the station operator. Give my name as Ian Curtis. I tell her the Chief personally told me to call him. After a minute of waiting, his voice comes over the line. I slide in a quarter into the slot.

"Yes?"

"Hello sir, I found the tape you were looking for."

"Did you watch it?"

"No. I just found it in our backroom. It looks like yours. I can send it to you."

"No. No. I'll be right down."

"Yes sir."

"Don't move, you hear me," real prick-like.

And that's when I rally the guts to do it.

"I don't have the tape at the store."

"You said you found it in the backroom."

"I want to know who she is," in an almost falsetto, my heart trying to push its way down into my nuts. "I want to know who the girl in the video is."

There is a real long pause.

I drop in a dime.

"What the fuck is this? Are you crazy?"

"I just want to know where to find her."

"Give me that fucking tape, kid. I can make your life real miserable real fast, you hear me?"

"Sure. But please. I have to know her name."

"Why?"

"What do you care?"

"Then what do you care?"

"Just tell me where I can find her, and I'll gladly give you the tape."

"I will be at your store in fifteen minutes. You either give me the tape then, or things are going to get very bad for you."

He hangs up before I can say I won't be there.

I book it back to the store, spot Evan with a customer, and keep trucking around the corner. No one is looking my way as I pull down the fire alarm next to this yellow nuclear shelter sticker. I walk on like nothing is happening. By the time I am driving out of the parking lot passing all the BMWs, there are still no sirens; the alarm is still ringing and many people are out now on the sidewalk looking around. Pretend to be as confused as they are as I pull out of the lot, hitting 495 as quickly as possible. Do the speed limit and after a few miles it is clear no one is following me. Pull off an exit with the arches, and grab a twenty-piece McNugget with barbecue sauce and a large Coke at the drive-thru. Should have also gotten some fries. I go back to my place and call the store. The voice I've heard before says hello. I hang right up. After pulling all the shades together, I lie down on the floor, grab the comforter from my bed, and cover myself up like Gene Hackman in *The Conversation*.

The blanket doesn't cover the banging on the door, ripping me awake. I lay there terrified out of my brains, hoping it will finally stop. But when I hear the key slide into the lock, I know it is over. My father walks in with the Chief behind him. I sit up and show my face.

"Henry, the Chief of Police is here," dad says with a strained voice. "He needs to see you privately."

Then it pops out: "Is my store okay?"

Chief looks at me for a second with his mouth a bit open like the ape he is.

"That's why I'd like to talk to you in private about."

"Sure, sure," dad says. "Okay let me... Well, I'll be in the house, okay?"

He leaves through the door and we both watch him out the sides of the shades walk across the driveway, pass the Chief's black Blazer, and into the dark house. His silhouette cuts across the kitchen window, unmoving, staring our way.

"You got one chance to give me that tape."

"I will. Just please tell me her name."

"Why?"

"Please."

"Fine," eyeballing me for a while. "Her name is Joelle Caldwell. Happy?"

I reach under the futon for the tape, grab it, then feel the barrel of gun at the back of my head. Everything inside me goes cold. I turn very slowly and emptyhanded. I notice the big bandage on the other hand. I just can't seem to look at what's in the other one.

"The tape," I cough out. "Under here."

"Get away."

I do so very quickly.

He pulls the thing out and looks at me.

"This the real tape?"

"Yes."

He slides his gun back into its holster.

"You ever tell anyone about this, I can make it look like you were killed in a robbery at your store. Or I can have your place shut down for any reason. And then what for you? Huh? So be smart and forget about this. Okay?"

He stands there looking at me with these crazy fucking drunk red eyes for about five hours. I try not to lock on.

"Who else saw this?"

"No one else. The only reason I saw it was I thought it was something else. But that is the right tape. Trust me."

"No one else?"

"*No one.*" Palms towards him.

"You've been warned, you hear me? Do not push it. I *can* get away with murder."

He leaves quickly.

I sit down on my bed trying to breathe. Slow. Slow everything down. Let out like this start of a cry, and then I stifle it. Don't doubt for a second that that crazy fucker could do anything he wants and get away with it. Everything in my head is out of order, spinning like the whole fucking universe is out of control. Pace around for a while, and put *Unknown Pleasures* to drown it all out. I lock the door and stick my desk chair under the knob. My phone rings a bunch of times, and dad tries three attempts at knocking. I just lay low and hope it all ends.

HENRY

There is that point between being able to control your thoughts and the moment the dream world takes you under. That is where I was stuck. Sort of like when they put you under with sodium Pentothal, like they did for my appendix. But when you go under what are the odds that maybe you never come back? That's the real terror. Not the pain that awaits you, but never facing it. Things float near my head, formless and soundless, but as real as could be. The fin is right about to break through the glassy flat surface. When Evan told me I should go home and get some rest because I looked like fucking shit, I finally relented, fell asleep at a red light, woke up to someone in a rusted out red Chevy truck flipping me off, and drove back to my apartment.

In bed finally, the bathroom fan giving me some familiar noise, a scene is shown where I step into a pothole full of gray water and get my pant leg wet. When you look out the window here, to me, it is as terrifying as that Henry's industrial blight of a world. There is no safety in his little room and there is sure no fucking safety here in the suburbs. He can get me anywhere.

It's Freddy's playground. Cheerleader and Most Likely to Succeed straps it on at night. Death can come from anywhere. Felt like this for weeks after I watched the *Day After* on ABC. What's going to stop those missiles from dropping down here on us? No Han Solo can stop the Russians if they want to go for it. End times I guess. I try to make some sense out of it all; the way she grabs his hair. The way she slaps his face; just have to arrange the pieces correctly. This mosaic is what shifted in my dreams the entire time I slept.

Dad caught me before he headed out to work. Hated to lie, but I need to remain above ground. Just told him the Chief was asking me questions about the break-in. He didn't buy it, and left in a big huff. He hasn't bought much from me since I fucked up while in college. Try never to think about it, but of course my brain pulls it forward every so often to remind me how much I suck. Just when I think it is the past, it drops by for another unwanted visit.

The old man busted his ass working two jobs and all that for me to go to college. He had enough saved up for the entire four years, with housing and books and everything. His mania all started when my younger brother died. Harry was five and I was six, and he was really healthy, I remember, then he was really ill. There were a lot of hospitals and a lot of bills. All that time and treatments and vomiting and all that awfulness wasn't enough to save him; he died in the house one night when I was at my grandmother's. Six months later, we moved to the place dad and I are in now.

Being that young I didn't really see how distant my parents had become to each other. There was nothing but silence in the house most times. That and tension of course. I really got tight with Evan's clan, and spent many holidays with them eating weird foods and not understanding a goddamn thing. I didn't care, I was happy to be a part of something. My mom is a big drinker and known to do things just to hurt the old man. After decades of battling, a few months ago she landed the knockout punch. Dad just keeps to himself as he always has, busy fucking toiling crazy hours that he doesn't have to work. How many nights he stays in his office until eight or even later, I don't even want to imagine. Walking into that empty house now must be like coming in and seeing it all crumble in front of you again. That night you came home to find the note on the piano where she used to give me lessons...

...But before there was this...

My first week of college I receive this letter in my mailbox from the Bursar's Office, saying I had some extra money coming to me due to overpayment and there was a check for $650 waiting down there. I ran down, got the thing, booked over to the student check cashing place and stuffed my pockets with twenties. Then I went to this kid I met in my dorm who said he had all sorts of connections. He seemed a little too over the top, and even though I was a bit unsure, it didn't stop me. I thought that he could secure me a half lid. I was going to triple my money, meet some chicks, lay some bread on dad, pay my own way, *and* have plenty to smoke.

Well the kid was an undercover narc they stuck in the dorm in case anyone is stupid enough to trust someone they met just four days ago. When the deal was going down in my room he grabbed the door handle, knocked the chair from underneath it, and in flood ten cops. Next thing I know I am on the phone to my old man, crying. He came up to Amherst and bailed me out of jail. His face showed no emotion. Nothing. But as he drove me back up north without saying a word, I knew what little connection we did have had been severed. My old man had done everything the right way his entire life. He served in 'Nam, injured his kneecap, received a Purple Heart, married mom, had two kids, and worked his ass off for every cent. Jesus, what more could he have gone through, outside of growing up in an orphanage? He is as straight as they make. And here I am facing charges and maybe even prison and his dream of my college education is now dead as his love for me.

The next day, using my college money to pay a lawyer, I sort of finally understood that this might be for real. My dad knew not to fuck around. This guy was an eagle, and had the whole thing thrown out on an entrapment rap, clearing my record. That was one of the reasons I could get a line of credit from the bank to help us out when we needed a little bit more stock to really fill the shelves here. I think my dad feels I'm a fuck-up, and probably thinks I am selling drugs again, and this is just a front and the Chief of Police is ready to take me down within the hour. No matter what though, people don't ever let you forget what you've done, no matter how much you've tried to change. You are tagged and that is that. Yet when I opened this place, dad was pretty fucking proud of me.

It was like for him maybe I had turned a corner. He was really impressed when the mayor cut the ribbon here. The mayor also cut the ribbon for the new dollar store in town that day as well. I know because his driver asked me if I knew where the place was. Nonetheless that was a real turning point for us after almost six years of him just getting sick at the very sight of me. He had to drive right by the mill to go to his work, so he'd drop me off there every day. On Saturdays, I either walked or biked. Back then he let me stay rent free, and that was how I was able to save every dime to finance this place. Then one day I walked in and let my folks know Evan and I had just rented the space. I figured he would freak, but he was like, my son the upright citizen... And now this bullshit. All that good mojo is probably wiped out forever now. I could see it in his eyes: You're up to something. But I'm not. I got sucked into this. And if I told him, he would either not buy it, not understand it, or he'd be completely freaked. My best bet is to just shut the fuck up.

I showered and went into the store to shelve returns. Even owning the joint never dulls the truly repetitive nature of work. But I do this for me and only me, so it is quite tolerable. In all these cubicles and banks and lawyers' offices and factories and mills and all that type of shit, man it is the same thing over and over and over. Ever worked in a mill or a factory? If the people don't drive you insane, doing the same thing for most of your waking day will.

We would pull these huge lengths of rug off these spools, align them on the rollers, and walk the thing down to the cutter. One guy on each side you feed the carpet into the mouth of this gigantic and mad hot machine. It takes in as much as it should, chops it, then moves the cut down the line. If you don't wear gloves and pull your hands back quickly, you will get serious fucking rug burn on the palms of your hands and between your thumb and forefinger. After feeding in the first fifty yards or whatever, you go back and pull the lip of the next one down. One fifteen-minute break in the morning, half hour for lunch, (unpaid), and one fifteen minute in the afternoon. My movies kept me company during those times. I remember working the Saturday the day the college class I should have been in was graduating. Dad reminded me about that all weekend, even though I burnt my hand badly that day, because I worked without gloves and had been completely shitfaced.

Most people who work those type of jobs use something either on the site or before and/or after their shift. The drunks think the pot smokers are lowlife hippies, and the pot smokers correctly think the drinkers are drunks. Saturdays in the parking lot was guaranteed to have at least two drug deals and three fist fights going on at any one time. It was all from jerks getting ripped in their trucks and talking shit about who can pull the most carpet in an hour. Those were the things that caused it to come to blows at the mill. The only thing good about the place was this one old stoner named Bill who sold me really good Thai Stick for cheap. He actually understood what I was going through, since he was wasting his life too.

"The only thing worse than working," he would tell me, "is not working."

"So I guess we're all fucked."

"I don't worry. World War Three is never going to happen. It's always going to be the same for us. It's one day after another really. So yeah, we're all fucked. Places like this grind us down. After a while you get like me and it doesn't even bother you anymore. I hope that never happens to you Henry. Always be able to feel the pain of places like this."

"Why the hell are you here, man?"

"I was a fuck up. I went to Rhode Island School of design for painting. Lasted the first year. Did nothing but smoke and drink and screw. Then I dropped out, bummed around for a while, got my girlfriend pregnant, started working here, got married, got divorced, the bills added up, and I just got into a comfortable rut here. Now my son is twenty-three and living in Seattle. He has nothing to do with me. I was working all the time to pay for his education and everything else. His mother raised him really. I was always here. And look now. You see what I am saying?"

And I did.

He was the only one happy for me when I left. Most everyone else didn't even know my name, and didn't own a VCR so I had no use for them. He visited the shop a few times, just to look around. Last year he ticket moved down to Florida to forget this awful place and live out his life on the federal dole; who can blame him? I never hear from him anymore; hope he's still alive.

The first person through the door, a bleach blonde Yuppie trophy wife starts complaining at me. Turns out she just can't figure out how to adjust the tracking on her machine. When you talk sense into them, it is almost impossible to not have anything but contempt in your soul for the whole lot. When I was done schooling her, the memories of last night were playing over and over on my mind screen. Every time the film ends differently: There's the one where he shoots me in my stomach, done in two takes; the one he kills dad first then beats me to death; the one he kills dad then takes me somewhere to make another film–that's the one that fills me with the most horror. That look of shark's hate he has; lurking in every corner of my mind now, howling away, pointing that gun at my face again, those beady fucking rat eyes all red and full of hate. We all know he is capable of it. He'd be delighted to know he's killing me every second of the day.

Evan came in two hours later, carrying a box of donuts on top of a large cardboard box full of videos.

"Thought I'd grab the new stuff now," walking into the back past me. "Jesus, did you sleep last night?"

I follow, but only for the donuts.

"Couldn't sleep."

"Well get some caffeine into you. Sugar too. Drink some sugar water, helps me get going."

I grab a chocolate chocolate, shovel it in, then drop a two glazed down my gullet using a Miller to push it through.

Evan's drinking right out of a 2-litre of RC. "I do miss New Coke, you know that? I liked it."

"I'm sure you could find some."

"Nothing, pulled right off the shelves."

"O."

"It had a bit of a dry taste. But I like that sort of thing and I can get away with murder you know and just let it go didn't give it a long enough trial run I think because don't push it you hear me Coke what do you care Coke and Coke and bring your hand out of there I have a loaded gun in your fucking face and I will blow your brains out and then probably fuck you and that is why it is better than old Coke."

I am sweating.

"You don't say," hustling into the bathroom.

And even as I am on the can he starts going on about how great it was, and just one flex on the finger, one nervous motion, and that is it. And for what? Piece of shit. And who the fuck is he to tell me anything? He knows I know and that must be killing him. He's the one who's pissing his pants, not me. Fuck him. Take a bottle of Jim Bean from behind the toilet and take two nasty, throat scorching pulls. Cool my esophagus with a few tokes off a roach in my pocket. Transformation is complete. I came busting out of the shitter like you know who out of a phone booth.

That explosion helped me finish off the dozen while lecturing on how to correctly pronounce ixitachitl. Then we started to discuss which is better, *Keep on the Borderlands* or *In Search of the Unknown*, both seminal modules. Evan brought up in *Keep* there are all these clerics, but no church around; or is it the other way around? I think the flaw in *Search* is that for characters who dominated the lands and had the undead build their dungeon, they were pretty weak and had little treasure. It would have been a much better higher-level adventure, really. Easy to convert though, and that is the brilliance of it. Lenny showed up around the same time as our two part-timers. We put them to work, got our heads right, and I started DMing S2: *White Plume Mountain.*

We were having a good time until I dropped right out of my high, and the Chief showed up in every corner again. I ended the game at an okay spot, but maybe a bit too abruptly. We all went into the alley again and got balanced. Lenny came back inside to change, then off to work for a nap. It took three more trips into the alley to keep me focused that day. After that I did all sorts of cleaning inside and stocked the shelves until everyone else split.

When I blinked again, I was turning the key and mumbling, "no goddamn it no," but the sound and fury was in my head in the form of this burning noise and it was drowning out the radio. Turn up the volume, but nothing. Turn it off and it still comes in through the rolled-up windows. I scream my throat so raw that it takes two chocolate shakes from McDonalds to calm it down. Finally, sitting in the parking lot looking at that red and yellow sign, full as a pig about to be slaughtered, I just said fuck it.

It was trash night on her street, and there were a bunch of bouquets of flowers sticking out of one of the cans. The sight of them sort of made me sick. There's Travis Bickel burning all those flowers in his dirty sink, thinking he might have stomach cancer. And there he is on the phone; so painful that even the camera has to look away. A car turns its lights on in the driveway, and my heart goes sideways. I split right away and head back to my apartment.

I said no for a while, but then it was too much again and I watched the vid over and over, freeze framing it on her face and just to make sure I've missed nothing. My soundtrack never stopped. Didn't jerk off; didn't even get hard. I just looked at her doing whatever she was doing and tried to figure it all out. After a while, I laid down on my bed and stared up at a Debbie Harry's thick, red, lips staring down at me. Now I had found my own screen, and was burning to stick my head into it. As the darkness took me, I could see those eyes flickering light, but then it bends and I see them going empty and his hairy paws around her throat.

"What do you think of this tie?"
     "It's gay."

"It's not gay. The guy from the Cars wears one just like this."

"He's gay too."

"Maybe he should be more like your boyfriend Ian Curtis and hang himself in his kitchen where his wife and kid can find him."

"You see this is where you don't get it," shaking a coconut donut in his face. "That action made him more pure than anyone almost ever-him and Van Gogh," pointing at his skinny tie. "You think Alex Lifeson would die for his art? When Ian did that, man, he proved he meant every word of what he said. Pure."

"Pure asshole is what he was," throwing his near empty Fanta can at the trash barrel. It bounces against the wall, sprays whatever soda is left all over, and hits the floor. "Meh."

His tie is supposed to be a Van Gogh Starry Night print, but it's so thin, it just translates as a bunch of blurs. We had this art teacher in high school, Miss Wolbanks, she was in love with the guy. One whole class she turned off the lights and made us imagine what it was like dying "under the sun" like he did. What it was like when he shot himself, and bled out in a cornfield, waiting for his brother to arrive and say goodbye. I remember we did it on his birthday, whenever that is. We always got good grades in that class, because we bumped into her one day when she was buying some bud from The Hippie.

Evan fiddles with his tie as we play *Dungeon* in an hour before opening. Lenny usually needs to show up at work at the bell, just to make a good appearance at roll call or some shit, and so he never makes our morning games.

"The girls go wild for these ties, trust me."

"Thanks for the advice."

It was advice I didn't take, since that very goddamned night I found myself sitting in my car across the street from Joelle Caldwell's house, wearing a pair of blue jeans and a black *Unknown Pleasures* t-shirt. The place sat up on a hill, white stone, long and with plenty of windows. The empty trash barrels lay on their sides at the bottom of the yard. Fog was rising from the lower part of yard. A couple of cars were in the driveway, almost completely hidden. I sat there thinking about what to do, and how to go about it. But then this news van starts coming towards me from behind.

"What the fuck?"

Turn it over and put it into drive.

Blue lights kick on all over the two cars in the driveway, and before I knew it, they were pulling me over.

Two big fat cops get out of the car and walk up on me hard.

Trying to silence my heart.

"What's your name?"

"Henry Hanks."

"You have some ID on you?"

"Yes."

"Let's see it."

Trying not to wig out. Trying so hard to not wig out. No idea what is going on.

"Why were you sitting outside the house, sir?"

"I don't know."

"You don't know?" he's got stubble all over his monkey face, and looks like he wants trouble.

"I just. I don't know."

Out of the car I go, and they've got me spread against the hood.

"Well, I don't know."

"You don't know?"

"No."

"I think you should come down to the station with us."

And that's what breaks the spell.

"Am I under arrest?"

"No. Just come with us."

And by now the whole neighborhood is getting quite the free show. There is a camera crew filming the whole thing. That might be saving me from a serious beating right now.

"I'm here to collect some overdue videos. I work-I *own* Metropolitan video."

Freeze for a moment, trying not to puke, knowing right then the Chief will find out everything.

"You want to collect late videos from these people?"

"Yes."

"After all they've been through."

"I didn't... What do you mean?"

He eyeballs me for a few.

"Get out of here and never come back. You got that?"

A newsman approaches me with a microphone and camera crew as I hop into my car and drive away right at the speed limit. I serpentine my way back to the store, staying off main roads. The whole time I'm praying my no one hears about this. What the fuck is it with these cameras? What is going on here? Park in the alley behind the place, which I never do because there is only one way out, but my car is hidden well. I run around front and let myself in. In the back I go into the bathroom, smoke half a joint, then shit my brains out. Too numb inside to feel anything. Hide my smoke and crawl onto the futon.

Evan wakes me up with the smell of some sort of Toastems. After eating, I shower in the bathroom, then yank a promo shirt for *Day off the Dead* off the t-shirt rack. Slap the price tag on my ass. *Day* is actually a fairly disappointing film. Overlong no matter what version you see, and the acting is quite bad in some spots. *Return of the Living Dead*, which came out against it, is a far superior movie. Amplas was amazing as Martin-But that doesn't matter now. The fear those cops can send through your body is intense. If a shark took a human form it would be a pig. Their terrible mojo is something that's hard to disperse. But that's what they want, isn't it? All of us to just knuckle under. I think those cops looked at me and knew I was the real deal and not afraid of them. But then there is that great white who's already smelled my blood and tasted my fear.

I feel that post-cop shell shock for a few hours until I hear Evan yelling "holy shit!" from the back. I run in time to see on our 12-inch black and white TV is me getting into my car, a microphone shoved in my face and then me driving away. A young man had been pulled over and questioned by police. It seems the man was seen casing the home of Joelle Caldwell, who last week was stabbed to death and left in a trash bag at Hampton Beach. After questioning, the man was released. Her latest yearbook photo is on the screen. Not her... That's not the one... What is this?... Police will not say if the man is a suspect. The license plate of the man's car was registered to-and I flick it off.

"What the fuck, dude?"

"Dude, I was there to collect some overdue rentals."

"At night?"

"That's when people are home."

"A bit late, no wonder why they called the cops."

"I wasn't *casing* the fucking place. I went there to get some stuff and pulled over the side of the road to make sure I had the right address. I didn't see the cops sitting up there. Next thing I know they are pulling me out of the car with guns drawn and shit. Notice they didn't show that."

"They pulled guns out on you?"

"Can you believe that? Right to my head."

"What if the Chief finds out?"

"I dunno."

"Well he probably already has. We gotta think of something."

Then the phone rings and we both jump. On the line is my old man, which isn't much better. I tell him I was pulled over in front of the house, but I was cleared. I went there to get a whole stack of movies that she rented and didn't return. Imagine how I felt not knowing that she was a murder victim.

"Not just a murder victim," the old man says. "She was ravished as well. Just a senior in high school."

"That's just awful."

"Well, okay then Henry. Okay then. Um, I have to go to work now. Will I see you tonight?"

"I'll be here late."

"Well when I see you again we can talk."

"Okay, but there isn't a lot to talk about."

"Really?"

I spent the rest of the day doing nothing but answering questions from customers about what had happened. Thankfully the mother was refusing to speak to the press, so no one could really say I wasn't telling the truth. It was easy to fool the people who didn't really know me, since I had probably shown up at their house looking for overdue rentals. They seemed to buy most of what I was selling them, at least it seemed so, mainly because I kept the information to a minimum.

There was something going through me that night, compelling me to leave the store. Nothing like that had ever pushed me to leave my Shangri-La, but whatever this was, it was nasty and pushing me out there. I really didn't have much of a choice. Soon I was back at my apartment. It was waiting for me like I knew it would be. I pushed the button.

"I told you to not push things," the drunk meanness is everywhere in his voice. "You got fucked and guessed who fucked you? You've been warned. You've *been warned*. Now do anything else, and *you'll* be the victim of an unsolved murder."

The next morning both the Electrical Inspector and the Building Inspector from City Hall were down going over every fucking inch of my store. Evan hid our stash in one of the fifteen pockets in his parachute pants, and didn't stop pacing the whole three hours those assholes were here. We were given $375 in fines for the biggest bunch of bullshit, including having the wrong outlet for the refrigerator in the back room. That peasant even dared unplugged it. I did the opposite as soon as he left, but our staple of frozen goods was starting to sag. We were left with only one choice: Beggars Banquet.

"What the fuck could this be about?" Evan said over his paper plate of Steakums and Cheese Wiz.

"Got me. You know maybe we are supposed to, you know, like at Christmas time, send these guys something."

"Maybe."

"So maybe this Christmas time we pay off."

Evan sucked on a two liter of Jolt until the bottle collapsed on itself.

"Man, that is *good!* But this sure as hell ain't about a Christmas payoff." And with that he went out to the front.

"What does that mean?"

Customers were flowing in steady stream, and the questioning was far less frequent. Joelle was already yesterday's victim, and people were far more excited to talk about the season the Patriots were having. To not slit my wrists, I just decided to believe that the inspectors were just a random event that happens to local businesses from time to time. Told myself that over and over. But the next morning as the Sanitation Commissioner was down here checking out our plumbing, and because we sold candy and micro-wave popcorn bags, he nailed us for not having a permit to sell food. He also fined us for litter in the alley, none of which was ours. Evan started raving he would call one of his 300 uncles. The guy, who looked *just* like Mr. Drummond, smiled smugly and walked off.

"I mean, what the fuck is going on?" Evan said, driving one Hot Pocket down after another. "Is this because we didn't give the tape right back to the Chief? I mean you gave it to him, right?"

" *Yeah.* I was heading back to the store and heard that fire alarm going off. So since I had the tape at home, I ran back to get it. Then when I was about to leave back for the store, the Chief showed up at my place."

"He knows where you live?"

"He probably knows where we all live," sliding the last forkful of the orange cheese into my mouth.

"Jesus man, this is a royal fuck up. I thought he would be nice to us. I mean we know he's a faggot and all and kept still."

"He only knows that I saw that tape. No sense bringing you in."

"You're a true pal. That was on my mind. But let's face facts, I'm guilty by association."

"But we can't just let the guy shove us around until we're broke and out of business. Then what? We gotta do something," I said sitting down on the futon, and right on top of the back cover of my *Monster Manual.* Why they ever chose Quasit as the example...

"The best something to do is nothing. Pay the bills and if this is a warning then, that is all there will be to it. Right?" he said.

"I guess so," looking at the amazing Tramp drawing of the Rakshasa.

Evan walked over to the boombox and slid the ca-single of Rush's *Subdivision* into the boom box. He has the album, yet he *also* buys the single, which is on said album, because in his head this is the way he proves his love to his rock gods. If computers made music it would sound exactly like Rush. It is the most precise, perfectly played music you will ever hear–but without one goddamn drop of human emotion. Maybe that's why all the engineers and computer geeks love them so much. I prefer hearing someone who might not have that great a set of pipes, like Ian Curtis, but you can feel everything he says. Take *Isolation*, he knew what being all alone around people is really like.

The whole vibe had changed in the store. Everyone who walked through the door seemed to be against us. People were bitching we didn't have what they wanted, especially since *Nightmare on Elm Street II* was hitting the theatres on the first of November to keep the holiday rolling, and people wanted to see the original again. Guys who usually rented decent stuff were taking home terrible shit which made me sicker. I saw people I liked a lot going home to watch *The Karate Kid*. If any kid ever needed a beating it was the Karate Kid. Plus Arnold from *Happy Days* is in it; not exactly DeNiro and Peter Boyle here. And these people were either so pompous or overjoyed to get this shit, that it really started to wear me down.

By lunch I had to lock myself in the can with a couple of Millers and a joint. Evan went out and got some microwave hamburgers which tasted like someone shit on cardboard and put it between a stale bun. I ate it anyways, coupled with some near frozen Mountain Dew. After that I killed a fatty with Evan and the rest of the day fought back, scraping against my skin hour after hour. After we rang out, Carrie came by and picked up Evan. They asked me to go to get something to eat, but I was too done. I brought a copy of *Ten Little Maidens* from behind the double doors home with me. Before getting to my place, I stopped and picked up 40 McNuggets and two large Cokes. Took it all to the apartment, set my head straight, and did what I had to do to survive the night.

When I got out of the shower, the news was on and there's the Chief in front of some reporters.

"We have obtained an arrest warrant for Jo-Anne Caldwell, the victim's twin sister. Ms. Caldwell's whereabouts is currently unknown."

I'm thinking, well at least people will stop bothering me with that bullshit. They didn't. Everyone I see it telling me how relieved I must be. I tell them the truth: I never had a thing to worry about. These dickheads did represent cash to me though, so I suffered them with a smile and the old aw-shucks shrug. We were stacking the rentals back as fast as they came in, and in the horror section, they went right back off the shelf. In the later afternoon and evening more of my types were coming in, and they all knew me and didn't bug me about nonsense. There were about four of us in the corner that night and we were really getting into some deeper themes in *The Brain That Wouldn't Die*, when Evan flicked the lights for a five-minute warning. The emptiness just took me right there. Everyone got what they had come for and then split. About an hour later Evan and Carrie left. Then there was only me, and all those hours until the sun rose again, when this place would probably be safe again for me.

I went into the alley, got straight, and that's when the truth started coming to me. No way was I going to take this abuse and not do something. The Chief seems to like to get fucked, so why not do some fucking? I drove back home slowly and really thought things over listening to the entire *Unknown Pleasures* album. By the end, I was ready to do what needed to be done.

Pull out my tape recorder and slide in a new Maxell Gold. Let the video play until he's really getting his ass hammered. Push the red record and black play button down together and watch the tape start to move. Record about three minutes, stop the machine, then place everything back. Take the tape recorder into the car, then drive to the movie theatre off 495. There are still some cars, as a late night showing of *Fever Pitch*, starring Ryan O'Neil and *King David* with Richard Gere are still underway; two sure fire classics. Not that anyone in that place would know a goddamn thing about film. I watch the drones trudge out slowly. Five minutes after the last one crawls away, I walk up to the payphone next to the empty cashier's window and dial the police station.

The operator picks up and I can feel the bile shoot up my throat, burning. I ask for the Chief's office. She lets me know he isn't in, but I can have his message service. She connects me to that, and his rough voice comes on; thinks he's some almighty fucking deity. When the tone sounded, I hit play on the tape and let it rip into the receiver. An energy fills me. Nothing I've ever felt before. A white bolt streaming from the tape recorder, through my arm, down the phone line. I am completely wired in. It's better than *Scanners*. I stop the tape, hang up the receiver, and click the tongue until I get a dial tone. Drop the thing off the cradle and run like a motherfucker to my car. I drive off slowly and try to not think about anything.

He must get into the office quite early, because Evan calls me at my place the next morning and says the Chief is in a car across the street from the store, watching the parking lot I use. Drive the long way and park in the other public lot. Keep low and take some side alleys. See his car and I walk up bold as a motherfucker to the passenger's side of the car. His fat face whips around when he sees me in his mirror coming at him with purpose. He slides the morning paper off his lap, showing me a sawed-off double-barrel shotgun.

"You must have shit in your head."

"You set me up. I never did anything to you. I kept quiet. And yet you sent all those inspectors."

"You put that on my *work machine*, you little *cocksucker!* Someone else could have heard it!"

"You're trying to put me out of business."

"So, fucking what? That could have ruined me, you little piece of shit."

"Just leave us alone, okay? We're done with you, be done with us. You got a good laugh on me. Now we're even."

"You try anything else you little cock sucking faggot, I will do you in. You know what I mean?"

Nod slowly. There is a tinge of desperation in his eyes. And that's when I know who's really ahead here.

"There any more copies of anything?"

"Nope."

"I know where you live."

"You do. But maybe you don't know where every safety deposit box is in town."

He tenses up completely, a savage red rising through his irritated and poorly shaven face.

"Don't fuck with me kid," raising the shotgun at my chest. "I swear to Christ you little bastard, I will kill you."

I back away from the window, and he slowly slides the shotgun onto the passenger's floor, never taking his eyes off me. He nods hard my way, then drives off quietly. I run into the alley between the buildings and throw up in front of two guys in business suits snorting something off a key. They back up, check their pants, and keep on doing their thing. I walk over to the store, wash up in the back and smoke a full stick on the can. I am out of mind, and my eyes may be bleeding. Evan keeps knocking on the door saying I am Bogarting, and I keep telling him to fuck off.

"Don't be a weed hog." That's what I hear in the can.

I drop hard onto my-onto my knees-onto my knees and vomit violently into the can.

"You okay bro?"

Let the rest just drip out into the bowl.

"Yeah. Hoping this joint will calm me down."

"Doesn't sound like it's working."

"Give it a few," clearing out my nose.

I stayed on my knees, watching the blue whirlpool vanish with some brown stomach shit that is pure acid.

"What the fuck am I doing?" echoing back at me.

The water started to rise again, a nice sky color, but still full of shit. I closed the lid and sat back on the top. I would have to loop something on my screen to blackout what the fuck just happened to me. I didn't want it to be what it was, but I figured I'd use the time trying to decipher it some more.

Is this really what I wanted when I fought and fought to become free? Someone destroying it all for me. Things had to be done and things had to change. No more guns in my face. No more of this knuckling under to a guy who takes it up the ass. I'll find her, or I won't. Her face looks out with those dead eyes from this wanted poster, the words Dead or Alive printed in red.

Out in the front Evan is talking to some Yuppie with a Patriots cap on about how much he is psyched for *Nightmare on Elm Street 2.* The original still isn't Craven's best; it's no *Last House on the Left* or *The Hills Have Eyes.* Not recommended for families. More people like to talk about horror and cult films during this month, and this is the time to recruit those who are ready into some real great stuff. Coffin Joe movies, the original *King Kong,* or *Shivers* or *The Corpse Grinders, Scanners,* or some of the great Hammer films. Sometimes you get one or two, but mostly you get people who won't rent *Night of the Living Dead* because it's shot in black and white.

By noon I am drained as a person can be, and tell Evan I am going home for a while to sleep. Once back in my place, I get out my Polaroid 600 and the video. It takes some fine tracking and just the right angle with my finger over the flash to get three out of the eight for my use. Hide everything again and crawl into bed, scared as shit, but ready to turn it around. A little after six I wake up, shower, and head back to the fort.

Evan is at the counter reading the paper.

"Just reading about that murder they thought you did."

"Shut up about that, faggot."

Landing a solid left hook to his left bicep.

He shoots one back, but I saw it coming days before the fucker even launched it.

"She was really hot, this Joelle chick."

"Dude, she's dead. So shut the fuck up. Seriously, man."

"Still, I mean look at her," holding the paper at me. "Nice body."

"Dude, she's *dead*."

"You don't jerk off to someone who's dead?"

"Not one that I was ever a suspect in her murder."

"It is a unique circumstance." Rubbing his arm: "That fucking punch hurt, queer bait."

This time he gets me right on the v of my left triceps. It really fucking stings, but my face remains blank.

"I don't jerk off to anyone who is dead," he goes. "Standards and respect, right?"

"No. Once they are on that frame of film, they are forever. Forever like that, and no matter how old Marilyn Chambers or Ginger Lynn or Joy Bliss ever get, and even 100 years from now, they will still be perfect on that screen, and open game for me."

"I dunno. They are dead. They're just not here anymore."

"They certainly are. Right there on the screen. Eternal man. So if they aren't on film, then what? Maybe they stay in your head. Maybe they fade. Mostly they start to fade real fast for me. Tape and film, man. It's where it's at. Lon Chaney can never die."

We nuked up a couple of Swanson fried chicken dinners, starring mashed potatoes, apple pie, and some vegetables I don't eat. After that I go in the alley and smoke. Maybe letting it go is the best way. Go looking for this girl and for what? What do I care. Just let it all slide by and things will be fine. And that was my thinking now. Inside Evan announces he is leaving to drop off the deposit, then meet some girl at the mall. I am wondering if it is the same girl he dated when he and his family went to Israel for three weeks when he was sixteen. Sadly, they both lost each other's addresses, and contact just faded right away.

I vacuum the rugs twice, and doing this bullshit work doesn't bother me one bit, because it is for my benefit. But even all this high-powered sucking won't drown out that noise when it fires up out of nowhere, driving my fillings like pistons straight into the crimson nerves. The pain blitzes through my skull. I go into the back and try my best to get myself under control.

Nothing works.

My head is throbbing, and I now know I just can't help myself. Hit play on the VCR and *Creature From the Black Lagoon* comes over the screens. Sit on the floor and watch it until the swimming scene. It's the most erotic sex scene that involves no sex ever shot. The first time I saw it I was pretty young, but I got it. Sex without sex... Sex without touching and sex without disappointment. Something real that is not really real. That is fine with me, but just wish sometimes that it didn't have to be like this. That it could be real. So much of this I just don't want.

Just like I don't want to be walking out to my car, but I am, knowing nothing can stop me.

Then something stops me–my car's windshield. A dull orange brick rests dead center in the middle of the glass web. I try pulling the brick out, but the whole deal sort of moves forward, dropping right onto the front seats. I take anything of value, brush it off, then haul it back to the store. I leave it all on the table and then get right to smoking. Looking around the room through bleeding eyes I see my bike, and then everything pulls at me all over again. Find a pair of black leather gloves in the desk and wear them as I pedal through this frigging cold-ass night.

I've got a black baseball cap with a Misfits logo I painted on there last year. It's really the Crimson Ghost, one of the best of the RKO serials, but it's now linked forever with this amazing band. The Avenues are about three-four miles from the store. Some of them are nice places; most aren't. In high school we used to ride on the bus right by this stretch of streets. Everyone said they knew what went on in there during the night. I'd sit and stare out the window, imagining it all. Covered lamps with red lights like you see in those Health Class film strips. Two sort-of attractive models on top of each other, the sheet or towel across his ass. Wouldn't that slow you up? A room, a room with a bed, a room with a bed and a wash bowl and a mirror where you can watch her do what you tell her and a room with this woman in it with these red red red lips and cock-hunger eyes just burning through your jeans as soon as you walk in. Your money is no good here sir. This is all for you. Your command is my wish. And maybe she means it and I am willing to believe it. Just like watching her or her or her on the screen, believing they love me. Believing they want me to cum in their hair or ram it into them. Believing more than anything that they don't really hate me.

These streets are full of loose patches and potholes, walled in by three story triple-deckers with these little black alleys between them. Everyone says that in those alleys are these doors that lead to brothels and underground motels and all that. Almost like the underground city in that awesome *Top Secret* campaign we played for a while. I was a damn good assassin, and Evan really did a good job running the thing. But there was nothing this scary, and I in the game, plus I was weaponed up. It is getting colder by the minute, and riding past all these places and people, people who are up so late at night walking around and watching every single thing that is going on, becomes far more terrifying than titillating.

Abort Mission.

I had to drive the car into the alley next to my store the next morning. Evan helped direct me in, and I parked with the windshield facing the road. I took the newspaper off the seats and threw them away. Glass sprayed out all over the place.

"You think..."

"Probably," I said. "Man, I hope he knows we get the point."

"Should we call him or something?"

"*No.* No not at all. Let's just keep our mouths shut. Not even Carrie should know anything."

"Yeah."

Evan took out his white and blue glass pipe and we spun it around.

"And we should tape us saying that if anything ever happens to us, that this faggot, pig-gorilla Chief is to blame. Then we lock it away somewhere."

"Even better idea. First let's call the glass company and get some Hot Pockets into us."

"I'll be right back."

Since we had to pay to have this alley cleaned up by the DPW, which they never did, then I might as well get my money's worth. I brought a broom out with me and swept all the cups and wrappers and dried up fries and onions and all the glass out of my car, knocking it around everywhere. Back inside Evan had already set up an appointment for my windshield to be fixed right where it's parked. He also had the ham and cheeses ready to go.

Then we got out the camera and filmed each other making a statement. We also revealed what was on the Chief's tape. Evan took the thing down to the bank for safe keeping. I sat there on the futon smiling away. I will control my own life, and this will show everyone who the fucking man is. Someone get tough with me, even the motherfucking man himself, well sir this is what you get. So everyone else better get right the fuck into line and realize that I have come of age. Everything laid itself out in front of me, down the line, and all I could see was victory coming my way. I had truly arrived.

Evan returned and we brought the place to life. The day was ugly and slow and dragged its nails all over our nerves. We took a long lunch and a few guys we knew dropped by, so we hooked up for a game of *Wizard* using some Grenadier AD&D minis from the yellow box, and the five games lasted almost two hours. That did help me a bit, but still I couldn't settle down. For the first time, I wanted to be someplace else but at my store. I'd be goddamned if I knew where I wanted to be. Locked myself in my car after everyone left and did some deep breathing. The smell of sealant covered the smoke stink nicely. Smells like the stuff they give you to relax in the dentist's office. I close my eyes with my back to the alley, to the sun, to the people. Try breathing deeply, but my heart is pounding out some crazy beat. Relax my eyes and just let it come. But no. My brain has locked the doors leading to that theatre, and no matter what I can't seem to reach my seat. Thought about getting really drunk and giving Evan my keys, but then he'd know I was up to something. Stay here and watch video after video and smoke up and just not think about anything. I was running out of time, and as the sun went down, I tried to think of anything to do, anything else besides what was swimming all over my mind.

Nothing else shouted it down, because that night I was behind that new windshield trolling the avenues again, looking at all the filth through an all too clean lens. There was a little bit of mist and fog on the roads, making it even more unseemly. People say the city lets the roads here go to shit so crooks can't get away that quickly. I was cruising slowly and dodging potholes and drunks weaving in and out of the street. On the seat next to me was what was needed for tonight. One had a shot of the Chief in the corner, his pig face looking right into the lens. I had taken a black Sharpie and blotted out his whole image. I drove around until I found a bunch of girls on a corner talking. One of them came over to the car, and asked me what was what. I showed her the picture.

"I was supposed to have a date with her. I don't know where to meet her."

She took the photo and showed the others. Nobody knew nothing. When the pack turned their backs, something weird ran down through me. Put the car in gear and took off out of that area. I went to the McDonalds off the highway and ordered a large Coke, two large fries and 40 McNuggets with BBQ sauce. There was some Go-Gos song playing on the radio. It was nothing but ambient noise to me. I got on the highway and drove up into New Hampshire for a while, started seeing too many Staties, then headed back to the Avenues.

On the corner of two streets right out of Ian Curtis's notebook, on the steps of a four-story hotel that dominates the area, I see this hot chick that wasn't there before. She is standing there all alone looking almost angelic, wearing a rabbit hair boa, smoking a cigarette, looking into space. I park at the corner and try not to run right up to her like some amateur.

"Hi."
"What can I do for you?"
"I'm looking for this girl."
She takes the photo and eyeballs it casually.
"Where did you get this?"
"I dunno," taking it slowly from her hand.
"Who is she?"

"Someone I think I used to know. We went to school. I'm, you know worried about her."

Our breath is visible, mingling into each other.

"For a date, you mean?"

"Well, you know, more for her safety and stuff. This isn't where she belongs."

"Sure. Sure. I know her."

"What's her name?"

"Whatever you want it to be. Now go up to the guy at the desk, pay him $100 and go to room ten. I'll get her to meet you there."

I am burning inside, trying to walk up the stairs. It is all too fast. Something makes me turn around, and I catch the little bitch catch her talking into her boa. My heart shoots out my mouth, comes around my body, under my shrunken nuts, and by the time I am jumping into my car, it is back into my chest, trying to get out again. Make about 100 feet before two undercover cars with their lights on block me in. They make me get out, ask me tons of questions, and run my record. Because I hadn't given anyone money, they can't charge me with anything real; they ticket me for loitering on the hotel steps. I drive in silence, trying not to think.

Found myself in dad's driveway, looking at the old man's bedroom light. He was watching television, hopefully nice and relaxed and not dwelling on mom, or me, or a number of other things he rightfully tries to ignore or just forget about. After an hour of watching the second hand move around and around, I tried to figure out what the fuck was wrong with me. Nothing really popped into my head. I did know that if the Chief caught wind I had been stopped in that area, he'd do something else; it would be whatever he felt the next step was, so I had to be ready. I went back up to my place and made a boot off the dupe. Then I found my old Johnny Pornoseed Tupperware porno container I stole from mom's kitchen years ago. It had those red sauce stains that never completely come out of the plastic. She never seemed to miss it. Yank out all the *OUI*s and *Playboy*s and *Hustler Letters* and toss them into the wastebasket.

A new level of need had been born, and stuff like that just won't do the job anymore. She had shown me the Nth degree. The point where there just is no further to go. I was as debased as a person could possibly be, and now the new age was crashing into me. Not like some hippie bullshit directed by planets and stars, but an age of flesh. Real hot flesh touching me back; allowing me inside it. That little flash sat me down on the floor for a while. I just don't know...

Placed just about everything pertaining to the tape inside the container, then pushed on the cover until it burped. I found some duct tape in my tool box, and wrapped the sucker up until it was completely covered. I went around back of my place, near the big tree, and used a rusty spade my mother had left to dig a hole near a large root knot in the ground. I buried the container, covered it and patted it down, dropped a heavy flat rock over it, and then dumped leaves everywhere to conceal the thing. The wind was intense, howling and howling at me like a Banshee just trying to force me into making a saving throw. Or maybe the wind is telling me this is the right thing to do, and the universe agrees with me. I know nothing anymore.

Went back upstairs and placed the master tape under my mattress, then laid down on the bed. Tried thinking about nothing, but nothing always shrinks into some rotten thought. Nothing was working, so I put *Here are the Young Men* on my VCR. Sat down on the can, fired up my bong, keeping the door open so I could watch the video. Looks like it was shot on Super 8mm, with the sound captured maybe right onto the film. Some parts are a bit dodgy, but there is a great version of *Digital*. Ian really does the epilepsy dance and it is something to behold. This is what it is like to be him; so talented, yet so flawed. You can't even control your own body. When it counted most, you lost control. How did you know it was over and you had to move on? What were you thinking dangling in the kitchen looking at the rinse-up liquid and racing further and further down that drain?

In the backroom, before opening, we smoked the rest of the dope we had in a makeshift Coke can bong, and then chucked the thing in the alley. I was resigned to a shitty week. When you know the fucking is coming, and there is nothing to do about it, there is no worse feeling. I'd be listed in the police log for my offense, and the whole thing with my Pop and I would be going full-force again. What could I tell him this time? He won't even buy the truth anymore. I stocked the shelves slowly as Evan blasted *Tom Sawyer* by Rush, doing all the stupid air drumming he could muster. I wish to hell I had *that* on tape; pure blackmail.

"Will you please wear your Walkman? Jesus Christ, *enough*!"

"This song is one of the three greatest songs ever."

"Will you just wear your headphones, *please*? Jesus, is that too much to ask, you fucking Christ killer?"

"What the fuck you acting like a faggot for?"

"Just... *Please!*"

"Fine. What do you know about music?"

"I know that song fucking sucks."

"You know nothing."

And into the back he trudges. Then there was just the hum of the overhead lights, which in a way has always been very comforting to me. It's about as close to real sunlight as I can stand. Carrie bought a tanning bed, which arrived this morning and is now in the back, waiting for its temple to be built. It sounded like an idiotic idea, but it will probably be a cash cow. The carpenters who fixed out door said they can build the room in a day. I focused my mind on what I was doing and very slowly let bleed in some ideas on how I could again talk my way out of a tight situation.

In the back Evan was sitting on the futon, eyes squinting under those huge lenses, air drumming like he was trying to save mankind. *Limelight* cries out from under his headphones. Once he finished his final drum rip I patted him on the shoulder. He dramatically brought down his phones; Mission accomplished.

"Okay, look man. I was really bummed out last night, and I knew we were gonna have to quit smoking for a while, so I wanted to get some real shit for a real night of sin. So last night I was in a place to get us a bag, and the cops showed up."

"Jesus Christ, you and your luck lately."

"No fucking shit, right? The dealer got away before anything went down. I had nothing on me but money, so there was nothing they could do. They ticketed me for loitering. I am nervous as fuck though that it will be in the police log and my old man will see it. Plus, you know..."

His face is a bit whiter than it was before I started telling him this. It drains upon the mention of the Chief.

"It was just a ticket, right?"

"Yeah."

"Let me call my uncle."

"Okay."

"So, you didn't get healthy, though?"

"Nope."

"There goes that too. What a day," throwing his hands in his hair.

I used the phone out front and called the newspaper. They told me today's edition was already on its way to the streets. Stood there for just a moment and tried not to scream. I marched into the back and began tossing the place in a panic, looking for any herb I could find. Evan hung up the phone finally and tackled me onto the futon.

"Get the fuck off me faggot."

I grab his left arm, get atop, and start whaling away on his shoulders.

"That all you got? That all you got you faggot? C'mon you fucking queer."

He punches me in the balls.

I slump off, nuts in hands.

"Pussy. That was pussy ass bullshit."

Evan jumps up, his glasses all over the place, yet his cement block of hair has not moved one millimeter. He sorts himself out, looking down at me on my knees holding my balls.

"What the fuck is wrong with you?"

"Why'd you tackle me you faggot?"

"'Cause you were trashing the place, you idiot."

"I am an idiot. The newspaper is heading to everyone's home."

"So wrecking the room is a good answer to that?"

"I dunno."

"You gotta clean this place up, man."

He's now looking at my middle finger sticking up at him. "Don't tell me what to do."

He's still rubbing his arm. "Just do it, huh? And get yourself together, will you man? You need to get laid, or something."

He walks into the bathroom to cool off.

"Okay Mister Man of the World. Think you're better than me, or somethin'?"

This was not a wholly unusual occurrence for the two of us. We've spent many hours of our lives punching, slapping, kneeing and head-locking each other into sleeves of bruises. We've been doing it since we were kids, so I guess we figured it was the best way to deal with most things. We met in a sandbox in Miss Crane's pre-school, and one of my first vivid memories is the two of us throwing sand at each other over a pale and shovel set. He cried way longer than me.

I straightened the place up a bit while still searching. Nothing. My nuts were going to hurt for a while, since he put the eight into a corner pocket by banging it off another ball. I straightened out my complete collection of *The Prisoner.* This guy I knew let me copy his master tapes for ten bucks a pop; well worth it. The covers were all Xeroxes of an original, with the episode number written in magic marker on the back. I stared at the wonderful covers of all the boxes: *April Fool's Day, Basket Case, Cannibal Ferox, Driller Killer, Evil Dead, Fun House, Ghoulies, The House That Dripped Blood, I Spit on Your Grave, Jaws, Kindred, The Mutilator, Night of the Creeps, Prophecy, Reanimator, Snuff* (don't bother), *The Thing* (both), *Underworld, A Virgin Among the Living Dead, Werewolf Woman, Xtro, Yor.* This moment alone was worth ten sanity points. Lay myself down on the floor, looking at the fluorescent lights, like dying Vincent staring up at the sun. If I croak, please let it be right here, looking at all these things that for whatever reason mean so much to me.

Evan stood at the end of the aisle: "He says you shouldn't worry. It's like getting a speeding ticket, he thinks it won't make the paper. Plus, they have no case. Anyone can be on those hotel steps. What's the fine?"

"Twenty-five bucks."

"I dunno. But your old man won't find out I should think. Pay with cash, or something."

"I can't go down there. What about the Chief?"

"He doesn't go through every ticket. You'll see. If it isn't in the paper, and it won't be, then no sweat. Just relax."

"So you think I should be cool, right?"

"Totally."

"Totally?"

"Totally, no fuckin' doubt."

"You sure?"

"As I told you just ten seconds ago, it will be fine."

This is far from our first conversation like this.

"Sorry I fucked up, man."

"Hey, it was for the common good."

Lying to him didn't bother me as much as it should have. Fifteen years of never doing it, that's a lot of credit in the bank. Around noon the papers went into their vending machines. With my throbbing nuts in my mouth I booked out to get a copy of the *Crier*. There was a mention in the police log that a loitering ticket had been issued, but only the time and place was put down. Intense relief washed over me. There was always the chance of the Chief finding out that it was me, but that was pretty slim by a mile. But if he did find out and saw where it was issued, he would know what was what.

"He's got other things to do besides go through every ticket issued every night."

"I guess so."

"Like having some whore fuck his ass and slap his face like a fucking faggot."

Evan seemed clear headed the whole day, and was mighty righteous to a crazy version of me having shown up. Twice I asked him if he was still worried, and he said the same thing: "It's all over. Don't even waste a moment thinking about it."

"So you're sure the Chief won't know?"

"Sure. Seriously, like I always tell you, just relax. Forget about it."

"Okay."

"Stop listening to all that Joy Division. That shit's not good for you. Like too much Pink Floyd, you know. Get your head set right, man."

And I know what he is about to say.

"Please. Please no lines from *Free Will*, please."

"Okay, but it makes sense, I tells ya."

"Just not now please."

"Don't worry. Worrying makes no sense. Man, you do need some weed. Maybe you should get a dime bag. If the Chief hears you got caught with that, he wouldn't care. He's got his own problems... Like being a fucking *faggot*," pointing at his ass.

I went back to my sections and sat on the green carpet, aligning the boxes. An orange leaf had somehow found its way in here, and was resting next to my left foot. No one was fucking with me and my head was nice and silent. There's Vincent in the cornfield waiting, that hot French sky burning his face, all those crazy colors dancing through him as his brain is shutting down. Did it all look like that to him then–just like he showed it to us. Is that what it is like at the end, and you always knew it? Looking up at the sky or looking down at the washing up liquid, it's all the same I guess.

Lenny walked down my aisle and we talked for a few. He felt my pain and not only sold me a dime bag out of his stash, *but also* lit me up behind the dumpster. We all got nice out there. Two of our employees were working the counter, and there was a need to maintain some level of professionalism with them. The three of us started splashing a little Brut over ourselves and things seemed covered. Then we got down to some nuked Howard Johnson frozen clam strips, Mountain Dew and the battle with the vampire deep inside the White Plume Mountains. I had a bunch of painted Grenadier Miniatures which looked killer. They were set down on a large piece of graph paper laminated with see-thru cabinet shelf paper. Blue Legos walled it out, and I had an excellent vampire figure from the *5002 Monsters* yellow box set in the middle of it all.

I played the creature as a raging blood mad maniac, who was ready to fight after all these years of thirsty sleep. Skall's illusions were useless, but he was able to ignore the monster's hypnotic gaze and get around for a backstab. Evan rolled a fucking one and all hell broke loose. The vamp started kicking ass until Lenny scored some big hits with his magic bastard sword. Then Baumgartner finally turned it around and did the deed with a 20 on a backstab. Fucker was wielding a newly blessed sharpened wooden torch. Drove it right into the heart from the rear. It was rightfully deemed an instant classic.

The game gave me a boost, as did the exit smoke I had with Lenny. He adjusted his tie and made his way down the alley, whistling the *Monster Mash*. I coasted out these feelings until the end of the day. Evan again was disappearing somewhere into the night, and I was all alone. Grabbed four Quarter Pounders, large fry, large Coke and two apple pies, then headed right home. I was on my last burger when I pulled up into the driveway. Slid out and walked over to my pop whose sitting on the back stairs smoking a pipe full of cherry Cavendish.

"Want an apple pie?"

"No thanks. That stuff is no good for you."

"I don't gain an ounce."

"You will."

"So what are you doing, Pop?"

"Nothing, just sitting out here."

"You, ah, you thinking about mom?"

"Trying not to."

"Yeah, me too, man."

"I don't blame her."

"O, c'mon man. It's not your fault."

He took a long pull on the pipe, then blew a few rings straight into the air.

"How's the store going?"

"This time of year is good for us. Did over five hundred today. Plus we have all the cameras and everything rented out for Halloween weekend. People just love movies on Halloween."

"That's great. Make sure you get the late returns."

We both stared at the ground for a minute and waited for it.

"What was the Chief really here about?"

"O. Truth is he left a tape in a recorder he borrowed. It was a confession and he needed it desperately."

"The police don't have their own equipment? They have to rent from you guys?"

"Evan said he ran in and said he needed one for police business."

"Strange."

"Yeah. He was pissed at himself and so he was less than nice. You know how cops are. And he was reading me the riot act about talking about it."

"Why?"

"I don't know, but he was flipping out about me maybe having seen it."

"Did you watch it?"

"No one did. You know I gave him the thing at the store, and then he showed up here all enraged. He's crazy, that guy."

"I read in the paper that he claims he is a former Navy Seal. Those are some dangerous people."

"Like Jesse Ventura."

"So just say nothing, okay? That's the best thing is not to pick at it. Just leave it be. You never know, he might appreciate your silence and throw something your way. You never know."

"You want me to stay up in the house tonight?"

"No. No, I'm fine. In fact, I'm turning in."

"Goodnight dad."

"Night Henry."

Went up to my apartment and pulled out my big plastic tub of video cases, but couldn't settle on anything. All the shit from these days made me tired as fuck, so I laid down on my bed and started digging Debbie Harry's bewitching lips. But where is your tongue to let me know it is really you. I was half way through the screen and half way home when the sounds started up again and she was right there looking down, her eyes locking right into me. No record was going to drown anything out. I just let it beat me up for a while, got up and walked around the place for a while dying for a smoke. I drank my last three wine coolers and paced some more. Wanted to call Evan, but I'd wake up everyone in the house, and it would be a thing. Settled on HGL's Blood Trilogy. The racket in my head just burning through me every three minutes or so. I know these films frame by frame, but they took on an odd alien form to me on the screen. They melted into one movie after another, forming a loop of blood and carnage all mixing in with this terrible sound just pushing me forward.

Right before falling asleep near sunrise, I watch the other tape again like Dekker does in *Blade Runner.* The Chief's red, red face, his blubbery, ugly body are soon just pixels on the screen to me. I am solely focused on the room and what I can discover through these pixilated black dots. Camera was set static, so there is little I can ascertain until the end when I notice this Black and Yellow jacket like the kids used to wear at my high school. It is way in the corner, but there it is, bleeding into the darkness.

I was at the public library alongside all the homeless people when the doors opened on Monday. Shot right to the section where they keep copies of old high school yearbooks. I started five years back, and hit on the last one, when I saw her face in a sophomore class group photo. Third from the left, next to a black girl with braces and headgear, there she was pressed in black and white sporting a sweater and skirt. Third from the left: Mira Jordan. I pored through the book and found no other photo or mention of her. How could you ever know how important you are, my harbinger of the new era of pleasure.

I went cover to cover in the one before it and found what I had missed, her in a freshman year class group photo. She was wearing pretty much the same thing. That body I know all so well just blossoming. Took both books and Xeroxed the photos in duplicate. All the hours playing *Call of Cthulhu* were finally paying off. Went through the last two weeks of newspapers to see if any other high school girl was missing. There were only articles about Joelle, with a short blub about a young man questioned for sitting in front of her house. If some white girl went missing, even a poor one, it would have at least gotten a mention in the papers. Then if this girl is not missing, does that mean she's alive? Dose she sit up?

Slid the photo in my jeans pocket. A type of calm washed through me. More like Novocaine. These papers became a codex for some cosmic cryptogram, or at least part of one. I parked across the street from the store and stared at the pictures. Jotted some notes down with a Bic pen on the back of the sheets, folded them up, and back into my pocket again. Walked across the street like a hitman in *Top Secret*. Maybe that would be the next campaign I'd run, with a video tape as the center piece of it all. A young girl, owned by a merciless senator, exploited for everything she is worth. There I am waiting in the closet with my garret in my black leather gloved hands. Let her really start screwing him before I move in silently and take him out. Would she stop? Would I?

Once inside Metropolitan I grabbed the phone book and looked up all the Jordans in town. There were ten, which was a lot more than I had thought would be around this place. Could call looking for Mira and see if anyone replies. If they ask, I say she has a movie out and it is overdue. No? She doesn't? She's only in high school? Terribly sorry. Evan walked in before I could start any calls. He was wearing this ridiculous Perry Frey, (I know this because told me so many fucking times), white and aqua striped long sleeve shirt and these god-awful almost turquoise parachute pants with about sixty pockets, and his perfectly chiseled hurricane proof top.

"What's with the long sleeves?"

"Fuck you. How are your nuts?"

"Why don't you open your mouth and find out."

"You would like that."

"You'll be back into your colored wife beaters from Tellos by November, don't you worry."

"I never worry."

Fucker knew that would get to me. Stared right at him until he shrugged his bony shoulders.

"C'mon, I went to Hickory Farms last night at the mall and got us a huge beef stick. We eat for peace!"

This makes everything fine with me, and we devour the whole thing like jackals. I partake in the Jolt cola, as is the custom of the Hickory Farms beef stick.

After it was over I said: "Did you go to Lauriat's last night?"

"No. I just went to Hickory, the Dream Machine and York Steak House."

"Who'd you go there with, big spender?"

"Just this girl."

"What did you play at the Dream Machine?"

"I got to Pizza Pasta on Punch Out. 'Ody blow! 'Ody blow!"

"Nice. The Sandman got you?"

"No. It was time for our reservation."

"You didn't fight for the title?"

"No. My guest told me I should do it, but you know, I was hungry."

"Dummy... *My guest...*"

"Steak was good though. Ate a lot. They got a good salad bar there."

Not sure if he was trying to impress. Nod and go back to my sections to straighten them out. About ten minutes later the mailman came in and dropped off three boxes and a few letters. That's when the ice really started cracking. We received not one, but *three*, cease and desist letters from two major movie companies and a TV network telling us that it was a crime to rent films that we either taped off the tube or bootlegged. They wanted word immediately that we had taken all measures to end this "piracy" right now. I grabbed a large corrugated box, yanked everything that was at all suspect, and locked it in the trunk of my car. When I returned, Evan was on the phone, once again, with his uncle. I shot-gunned a Miller and sat down on the futon with my hands still shaking.

"Okay," Evan said walking to where I was. "He said what we did was the best thing to do. He also said if anyone comes in and asks anything, don't say *shit*. Call him and he will be right down, or will send someone down."

"Fine with me. God bless your enormous family of lawyers."

"And as far as we are concerned, no such tapes ever existed, and don't talk about it, even with the regulars."

"Gotcha."

"How many tapes were there?"

"Seventy-six."

"O man."

"And you know a few of the guys who rent *Hill Street* from us are cops."

"Oh fuck, me. Let's take them out the computer even."

We had an almost brand-new AT&T Unix PC, which Evan was quite adept at using. Took him about twenty minutes to get all the titles out of the data bank. He then started looking around for any mentions of those rentals, and wiped them out as well. We took the printed up lists we had for customers and burnt them in the dumpster.

I handled the front as Evan got to work. Most of the people coming in were Yuppie types who are looking for something to keep themselves going. A few times we had a line; mostly guys holding porn chits. It took everything in me to focus on what was going on. The other side was piercing through, turning my mind into one Grand Guignol. Every night I am in there, eating desserts made by someone named Sar, watching these hell players throw the acid in my face and there isn't a goddamn thing I can do about it because this is where I *really* live.

Held out until Lenny came in after the evening rush, apologizing for not coming around at lunch, but he was sleeping in a closet off his office and didn't hear his officemate's wake-up knock. This is his plan: find a corporation to latch on to, do as little as possible without getting noticed, and then sort of have them underwrite your life. But, there is still a boss. And a schedule and bowing down to your inferiors, and fuck that shit one million times in the ass before breakfast. He had three joints on him, and slid me one. I was so nervous about being caught in the store that I hopped inside the dumpster in the alley and ripped it to nothing but a tiny white cone. Made sure everything was clear before I crawled out and went back inside. Trying not to be too piss-ass smelly, I found a 900-ounce bottle of hair spray in the back and gave my pants a once-over. It stunk, but half the people who come in here, and half who own this place, reek of this shit. When no one was at the counter, I went up to Evan.

Quietly: "This can't be about the ticket I got, could it?"

"No. I doubt it. I think he let the places know about us right away, and it took a bit for their legal department to contact us. We just gotta stay cool. It's like it never existed. Remember, the Chief owes us, right?"

"Lot of those were going to be big Halloween rentals. Not my fault I have connections and give people good shit. Man, the *money.*"

"I hear ya. But we gotta be cool about it."

"I guess I could do them under the table."

"*No!*" Waving like I just slid in safe to home plate. "No one. Not even Carrie. We just gotta ride this out and do nothing. Do nothing is the best thing. Next Halloween we'll do double. It'll all be cool by then. Trust me."

Lenny's smokes kept me out of my brains with trips behind the dumpster every 90 minutes. Still pissed about not being able to do what I wanted to in my own place, but when the Man sees you trying to be free, he'll do what it takes to break you. This machine we've instilled here is sick and constantly crawling, searching for people like me. If they can't force you into a factory or office, maybe they can just lock your ass up.

Back inside we plowed through a whole box of frozen chicken patties with mayo on hamburger buns in fifteen minutes. After our guest split, the store started jumping. Had to run the register and find videos for people, even though they are in sections by genre and then listed alphabetically. Despite the terrible kickoff to the day, we made some cash, and I remained as calm as I could. The Chief had flexed his muscles, and all we could hope now was that he was done with his part of the round. By the time I slid the fat blue envelope into the bank slot, I was wide awake. Time for a drive to go check out some of those addresses. Then it hit me to use the city directory like before. That's when I first noticed I wasn't remembering or focusing as well as I had in the past. But when your head is swimming in shrieking noises and your screen doesn't do it for you anymore, and you gotta get some new kicks real soon, or *else*, it's *really* goddamn hard to train your brain on anything else.

I went home and tried my hardest not to watch the tape by drinking a whole six pack of *Bartels & James* wine coolers and listening to *Substance* on my stereo's headphones. Then listened to *Novelty* over and over with tears coming down my face. Woke up to the white noise. Woke up at 6:06 a.m., took a huge piss, then slept until almost 9:09 on my bed, when some noise pulled me out and into the shower. Did I really sleep? The woman behind the radiator had been talking to me all night, but said nothing. Drove to the library, got the information I needed in about a half an hour, making it to the shop one minute before my usual arrival time. Took the address and checked it against the phone book, which paid off with a phone number. Now I was getting somewhere. Had to do it differently this time. The last thing I needed was to walk into another cop scene and have the Chief find out about it. Then I'd really have to up the ante.

In the back-room Evan was dancing like a braying ass to Rush's *Subdivision* coming out of the boom box. If there really is a way to dance correctly to Rush, this was not it.

"The only thing Geddy Lee ever did in a basement bar was write code."

He stopped moving: "Actually the one who is mostly like to write-"

I put my hand up. "I don't want to know. I have enough things in my mind bothering me."

"You still worried about those letters?"

"You know me."

"My dad said the same thing as uncle-"

"You told your *dad?*"

"Yeah."

"O for fuck sake."

"Don't worry. He likes you just fine."

"Except for me being a criminal."

"Hey, he is a lawyer."

"He still thinks the reason you're not is your association with me."

"So what? This isn't about him, right? This is about doing what we want, right?"

"Right."

"So chill man. It's all fine."

I did all the things we do before opening the store, and tried my best not to listen to Evan humming the entire *2112* album. There are times when everyone thinks about murdering their friends, and that day it was all about sewing his mouth closed with barbed wire *after* choking it with him; this assures me his bodily gases will not make any Rush like noises–although those would be far more human sounding.

The first person of the day came through the door, some drone in a business suit, and my stomach went sideways. Mouth burns of metal. Whatever this was I didn't know, but something had awoken and was very hungry inside me. It knew I would feed it. What if the Chief kept pulling his shit? He must not be so stupid to think I wouldn't do something eventually. Or maybe this is what he wants; me half-crazy out of my head, a joke of myself. It is so much more painful than just being shot in the gut. My heart just wouldn't slow down, and I just tried to keep to myself as best as I could for the morning.

Carrie came in later in the day with all the paperwork we needed from City Hall to proceed with building the room for the tanning bed. She had this *Frankie Says Relax* t-shirt on that was oversized, but those perfect c-cups were still popping underneath. Missed out. My timing, God damned it. I could smell her and almost taste her again. It would have changed so much.

Started setting up for the gaming session to get my head straight, laying out the maps, and putting up the screen. Some say that is the artist right there in the foreground, in front of the ghosts, red dragons, lizard men, wyverns, treasure gazing adventurers. He's got quite a piece of tail with him. Once I saw *Wormy* in *Dragon*, I was hooked. There is no one out there with his talent for fantasy art, yet who is he? The temple of the demon god, with those ruby eyes about to bring us thousands of gold, we pry them out. The Green Slime will not allow you to pass. The Giants all with that post-Ragnarok cockiness. There is nothing he can't do with pencil or brush. Recently his output has decreased. I look through all the new games down at The Dungeon a few streets away, but he seems to only be doing the strip now. Maybe it takes him that much time; sure looks it. I've written three letters to him, but never heard a thing. His art was what drew me into the magic of this great game. His imagination is what got me hooked.

First saw the box in a small store on the corner of a building not too far from here. I was down town getting a pair of steel toed boots for my job at the factory. Had to stop because one of these wicked coughing jags I would sometimes have nearly put me on my knees. Three days in the hospital later that year taught me to wear a breather while cutting the rugs. These phlegm squids would just drop out of my mouth no matter how hard I tried to fight them. That day I stood up with all these colors and spots dancing in my face. When that magic calmed down, there it was in the window: *Monster Manual, Players Handbook,* the blue box basic set and a bunch of painted led figures.

Went inside and checked out the game and asked this pleasant, curly haired guy what the whole thing was about. Walked out with copies of everything that was displayed in the window, six issues of *Dragon*, two sets of dice, some graph paper, and nine dollars left for boots. After returning home and reading through everything, I called Evan near midnight, and the next afternoon we played our first adventure *The Keep on the Borderlands*. After that my six-day work week became a lot more tolerable. Living in my head in that world. Countries and empires rising and collapsing, clearing out for the newer ways. That's where I stayed for all those years. And then it got me thinking: If I could pretend that I was something more, then why couldn't I actually be something more?

Lenny came in with three joints blended inside a red pack of Marlboros, so we all got nice in an alley. A little mouse was behind the dumpster watching us while rummaging through a not quite empty bag of Cheetos. He found a piece the size of a fat doobe. Everyone was happy. Inside a rush was occurring out front, so the two of us had to help out for a few. Lenny sat in the back room and watched the news on our TV. When things did settle down, we didn't have as long as we wanted to do a decent gaming sess, so we took out the *Dark Tower*, and played a game where no one won. The three of us had a quick smoke in the alley, then Len dressed and split. I stayed feeling good until about five, when the sun was down and the neon just wasn't that comforting to me anymore.

Tried cleaning the store's windows from the inside until there was not one streak. That took a little while, but even with *Videodrome* playing on the overheads, I was just putting off the inevitable. Downed three more beers, and headed out to the address I had tracked down. It was shocking to me what a shit shack she lived in, which was just like the rest of the triple-deckers here. Packies at both ends of the street. I went around the block a few times, navigating carefully around potholes, trash and people. And the scum were everywhere - in the road and the sidewalks, caterwauling like Hobgoblins and challenging each other, making deals in car windows; a black electricity running through the whole scene.

Knew deep down that tonight I could not go on; the world had kicked the shit out of me that badly. I was drained from worrying so much and famished for something good. It was just all too much right now. Headed to a better part of town and grabbed some Wendy's before heading home. Finished eating in the car, then walked back to my apartment so I could just stare at her on the frozen, strangely pulled apart image on a stained screen. I must have looked at that goddamn thing for three hours straight, those grinding, testicle numbing sounds never missing the correct place to jump in. There were already some wear lines on the tape, making all of this that much more despicable. I couldn't get enough. I know every action that happens at every second. I know where hands and feet are placed. I know the entire cruel dialogue of 76 words. I even know the color and length of the toys. But does she sit up? He doesn't touch the bed. Maybe it is what they call death throes. Let my eyes unfocus and see nothing but bodies so hungry for me. Reach my arms out as far as I can, but these ghosts love to stay just out of my grasp.

Sort of wake up at work where Carrie is ringing up some woman with way too much makeup on. She's got straggly black hair, weighs about five pounds, ten feet tall, with a face you just wanna tell to shut the fuck up. But Carrie is all smiles to everyone, even as this bitch talks down to her. The chick is renting three porns. "O this is a good one, you'll like it," Carrie says. I've specifically told her to *never* talk to customers about their porn. The relationship between renter and rentee, *especially* with skin flicks, is a sacred one indeed. The woman just nods away with slight indignation, takes her tapes and walks off, leaving us with no customers.

It's been a long time since I have been all alone with her.

Year or so ago she was using my place to study for her RN exam, since there are about 897 people at Evan's house at any one time. I came back with a big bag of McDonalds and found her lying on my bed, asleep with a book over those restaurant quality tits. I just stared at her, like the kid in *My Tutor*, and stayed that way for who knows how long until she opened her eyes and sat up, the book falling onto her lap. We said a few words, but for some reason she stared at me like I was guilty of something.

"What were you doing there?"

"Well, you know, I do live here, and I just walked in and found a woman on my bed."

"Not a frequent sight, huh Henry?" with this big toothy smile.

"Ha. Ha."

"I'm sorry."

"You want some McNuggets?"

"No thanks. You mind if I have a cigarette in here?"

"Yeah, man sure."

"Listen, I'm not a *man*," fumbling around in her pocketbook. "You and Evan always call me that. I mean, is that how you look at me? Like a *man*?"

"It's just a thing I say. I mean, I know you're a woman."

Carrie lights up on my bed and I can't help but watch her smoke. Those big thick lips. All that lipstick and mascara. Her eyes smile some cat-thought, and then it pounces just before I can speak.

"You *ever* have a woman in your bed, Henry?"

I put the bag of food on my desk and sat down in a chair facing my grub.

"Why do you ask?"

"C'mon, we're friends."

"You know I had a girlfriend."

"O her? That girl."

"Yeah. My old girlfriend Ginger."

"You ever fuck her?"

"*What?*"

"You ever fuck her?"

"What a mouth on you."

This blue smoke circles my head: "What's wrong? Afraid of me?"

"No."

"Can I ask you something?"

"What?"

"Well turn around please, huh? There, thank you, not so bad right. You have seen me before, right?"

I look at her knees.

"Are you girl scared?" tapping the ash into a red aluminum Coke can sitting on the floor in front of my bed.

"No."

"You're not a bad looking guy. You own a business. I mean, you could be quite a catch if you did something with your hair, and wear some better clothes."

"I'm doing nothing to impress anyone. She can take or leave me."

"Well, they're not taking you, kiddo."

There was this awkward silence.

"I'm sorry, Henry. That was mean. I just, you know, you're a good-looking guy. You should be with someone and be happy."

"I am happy. I'm a free guy."

"That's true. But aren't you lonely? How many of these tapes under your bed are porns?"

"I don't know. Not many."

"Don't you want something real?"

"Sure. Who doesn't?"

"Do you?"

"Yeah, sure."

"Have you ever had the real thing?"

I say nothing.

She smiles and drops her butt into the can.

"Come here."

I just stare at the floor; the smell of my food making me sick and anxious.

"Henry, c'mon."

"What?"

"Come over here."

Hard to focus. She shifts. I smell the food again, swallow hard. But now she's closer, blossoming up is orange and lavender, tobacco and softness off her mouth which moves right onto mine.

"You're a cute guy. You should be with someone you at least *like* the first time."

"I don't know."

"This is the best, trust me."

And everything is going so fast for me. She comes off the bed, locking those tigress eyes on me. Currents of all colors streaming through me. Carrie pulls me down, the book goes somewhere, her legs wrapping around my waist. I'm not ready and I know it and my heart is pounding away because she's pressing those tits against me; soon they are exposed to me, her shirt pulled up under her chin, pressing against my chest. She is a blur of warmth and taste. Soon we are down to our underwear and she kicks those legs up and my mouth is almost numb from sucking on her nipples, and she yanks off her panties. We kiss more as she takes my hand and places it between her legs. That first sensation of the pubic hair sends the signal through me, and even though she's got it in her hand, it softens right up before even feeling the wetness.

"You okay, hon?"

"Yeah, yeah, yeah, it's just. I don't know."

She uses her mouth for a minute until I am ready to scream out. I slide away and stand up.

"Maybe if we watched some porn, that would be-"

"-*What?*"

"I just thought..."

"O man," smiling. "I can see we are not into the same things here."

All the color left.

Stood there with a limp dick and a cold sweat. Maybe she knew what was what and gave me an out. The two of us dressed in silence, then I walked her to her car where we hugged and kissed before she left. It was a while of weird vibes, but we were tight friends again not too long. She also never told anyone about this, because had Evan found out, he would have been repulsed, and somehow would have let me know it. That wouldn't have done a lot for me either. I always have this secret love for

Carrie because of what she tried to do for a loser like me. Tried to make me one with the flesh. I was the one who failed.

"How many more days in a row you gonna wear those jeans?" fashion plate says to me.

"What? Huh? When the fuck did you get here?"

"Just got in and saw that state of your pants."

"What are you looking at my pants for?"

"Get some style."

"I will, when all my Z-Cavarici's come back from the cleaners."

Walking off: "Your pockets are all fraying."

Did that mean he knew I had the copies of the photos on me. I took a few deep breaths, and figured out that probably wasn't the case. No way he could know. Few days ago, this equals meltdown, but just having these copies on me made my head feel a lot quieter. My stomach was killing me though, and I struggled at times to stand straight up.

"I think I might have stomach cancer."

I sent Evan out for a few chocolate shakes, and manned the store by myself. Always felt that maybe someday we would open another one, with each of us running our own place. This one would be mine. This place, my bride, my true love and fuck you to the world. Then maybe we could have spread out all over the Valley and have one or two stores in each town or city. But now something had slithered into our little happy valley, and it had to be extinguished completely.

The rest of the day sort of blended its hours together. Lenny came and went, and finally people were being released from work, quite a few came right through our doors. The last kid of the night was a skinny, bowl headed teen in a Marvelous Marvin Hagler t-shirt and gray parachute pants with about three hundred pockets. We usually talk film, but not tonight, and he walked out with *Blood Sucking Freaks* and *The Corpse Grinders*, two choice selections.

Carrie drove Evan away and when they were out of sight, I slid $50 IOU into the cash register, pulled the cash out of the deposit envelope, put it in the draw on top of three of Evan's notes. The deal is all IOUs must be paid off by Saturday when we close or you can't draw again for a week. We were both perfect on payback. After sliding the envelope into the bank, I got in my car and picked up a couple of Quarter Pounders and a vanilla shake which was nearly impossible to suck up the plastic straw. I parked in the dark lot and ate robotically. There was no joy in this food today. A few cars away some black chicks were blasting *Crush on You*, and dancing away in their seats. The one behind the wheel caught me looking and smiled at me.

"Come dance with us!" she yelled.

Just nodded with this stupid smile on my face, turned over the ignition fast and took off. In my rearview mirror I could see her shrug, her friends never missing a beat. Tried to wave, but something wouldn't let me; the same something that took me back to those streets where these sub-humans had all the time to be hanging out on stoops despite the cold night and fog. Many cars were lined up on the opposite side of the street, waiting to go into an alley. It all just kept moving. Her building was a triple decker with a wooden stoop. Parked at the corner about ten yards down and walked into the vestibule. Saw her last name written in magic marker on duct tape next to a door bell, and froze. Whatever it was that dragged me here would now not allow me to push that filthy white button. My finger was right over that fucker, but... Why was I even there? What was it that I really wanted from her? My finger just stayed there hovering sideways, knowing it was never going any further. I ran back to the car, hit the gas, turn a corner and then there is that noise-hit the brakes with a stop sign looking right into my face through a very cracked windshield.

Hopped out and bent the pole back upright. The fucking thing was sturdier than I thought it would be, and way deeper into my hood than I hoped. Managed to get the thing straightened out and back upright. There were a few silhouettes in orange lit windows looking right down at me. Got back into my car, turned it over until it started, and got out of there fast as fuck. By the time I stopped driving I was in the alley behind the store bawling my eyes out.

When I woke up it was still dark and my neck hurt from sleeping in the car. I got the flashlight out of my glove box and looked over the damage. The grill was a bit dented and the hood more scratched than anything else. The windshield was fucked, and who knows if the insurance would cover another one. I exhaled deeply and went out front and into the store, then straight to the back. There was one Miller left in the refrigerator, and I shot-gunned it, then sat down on the futon with shaking hands.

Sent a page to this guy I used to work with in the mill. He quit the place and went on to make a ton selling to all the people there. His hours are 8 pm–4 am. I took one of our flyers out under the counter and slid it into an envelope along with three free rental tickets. Sealed the envelope and addressed it to Mira. Took me a while to have steady enough hands to write. The phone rang and I placed an order. I walked down to the corner, dropped the envelope into a mailbox with an early pickup, then went back to the store. It was a little bit past two in the morning.

The place looked pisser clean, but I vacuumed again and threw out some really old shit in our fridge. Evan is one of these guys who always saves like two bites of everything for this big meal later. You take all these little bits of meals and nuke them, and that is his Beggar's Banquet. Problem is he keeps them in the original bags or boxes and by the time he is ready to eat it all, half of it is really bogus; he eats it anyways. The fridge stunk of pure wretch, and I chucked all the bags no matter what their date was. The reward was two recapped bottles of Schlitz hiding in the back; pure hell to get over my tonsils, but helped bring me down half a quarter of a notch.

Soon I let in this sophomore year flunk-out in a leather vest, ZOSO t-shirt, black acid washed jeans and spotting some real Malcom Young level feathered hair. In the back, I give him fifty bucks and he gives me a nice fat bag of weed. He leaves without saying a word. Before smoking I stash the bag in a ceiling panel above the futon, then write a note on my hand in code about where it is hidden. Sometimes you can forget these things. Everything is slowing down, but way back there, I can hear all those words she said–all 76. I close my eyes, watch some fractals hatching and folding, then fade to sleep on the futon.

My morning started on the floor. By 7:45 I found myself at the corner of the street where I first called the Chief. The traffic was heavy and all the exhaust rising from all over made me want to puke. Dropped a dime down and punched in the number I had written on the back of my hand, below the code. The woman at the school said Mira was no longer a student there. I asked if she had moved, and the woman said she couldn't tell me that information. Found myself back in the store unsure how to feel. Couldn't tell what it all meant. There were a few hours before Evan was going to be here, so I had a smoke in the bathroom and dropped onto the futon to look at the photos again.

Twist it around and around. So many angles and hard lines; What does her position being second in the line mean? Did they intentionally put a black girl next to her? Or was it because the girl had headgear? Two of her fingers are curled up under her palm, exposed are three in a straight line. Read between the lines? No. Much deeper. Follow the course. Follow the straight path now and everything will turn out as it should. My plan was settled as I slid the photo into my pocket again. I wormed all over that smelly cushion, yet somehow sleep did find me again.

I woke to some fuck face kicking me in the shoulder.

"You forgot to turn the fan on in the bathroom. Man, that shit stinks."

"Not worse than the fridge did."

"You didn't throw my stuff out did you?"

"It was *all* bad."

"You *faggot!*"

"Your stomach will thank me."

"You're buying lunch today."

"Whatever."

I turned on the fan to shut him up, and then showered. I always had changes of clothing there, and today I went with an *Isolation* t-shirt and khaki pants. Only after I dressed did I notice the dark oval stain on my leg, but it was faded enough that no one would notice. A memory of when Lenny dropped his Jolt over me during an intense game of *Divine Right*. Beat him on some lucky rolls. I called the insurance company again and told them someone had vandalized my car last night. As soon as the receiver was in the cradle, Evan was on me.

"Someone fucked with your car again?"

"No. No. I slammed into a sign high man."

"Just be careful, those guys are hawks."

"I'll talk my way into a check, watch. Why should I pay on that? Fuck them, they got plenty of money."

He shakes his head, but I watch his unmoving hair.

"You got a gyroscope in there?"

"You worry constantly about all this mundane stuff, yet you're willing to commit insurance fraud."

"It's not fraud, really. I just don't want to pay on it and there is no way they can prove it didn't happen."

This was somewhat the opposite of what was going on about an hour later with the adjuster. He was a grayer Stacy Keach fucker with a Ronnie Best Boy haircut, gray suit, grayer overcoat lined in fur and these big Statie sunglasses covering half his over-tanned face. I sort of came to my senses as he was pointing to all the obvious spots of red that rubbed off from the sign last night. He also explained how a collision looks different than someone smashing your car, "even if it is with a stop sign."

I just stood there with my hands inside my gray Pony sweatshirt and looked at the ground.

"Listen up, next time you want to try and rip us off, do a better job, huh? What were you, drunk last night and hit something? Was that it?"

"What do you want?"

"Pardon?"

I looked up at him, but only saw myself and the dumpster behind me in his lenses.

"You asking me if I would take something for putting in a claim for you?"

"No."

"You sure?"

"Yeah, yeah."

He smiles and out comes this horse mouth of coffee and cigarette stained teeth, all just crooked enough.

"Ask me, maybe I will?"

I said nothing.

"You sure?"

Nothing.

"Last chance."

Nothing.

"Tell you what, I won't put in that you tried to commit insurance fraud, a crime punishable with up to five years in *prison*. But I am gonna make a note in your folder to consider cancelling your policy, and anything else you claim we will strictly investigate. You got that?

We also insure your store, you know? That would go too."

Nod slightly.

"Let me tell you something else," lighting a cigarette like he's Bogie or something. "Guys like you piss me off. Think you can fool me? I've been doing this since before you were born. Think you can outsmart me? No one's done it yet."

I have my doubts about that.

He smokes the whole thing pretty much looking down at the top of my bowl. He gets it right down to the butt, then flicks it into my alley.

"Smarten the fuck up. I'll be watching you,"

He walked away smart enough not to blow smoke in my face, but cocky enough to have tried it. About two minutes later the little faggot drove by without looking my way. I got inside my car and just sat there. The windshield was spider-webbed in the middle, but the driver's side was decent. Started the thing up and let it run for a minute or two. It idled okay, even though it had been needing a tune up for a while now. I shined the headlights and they reflected, low and high, off the dumpster. Turned it off and sat a while longer, getting different smells from all the spirit wrappers on the floor next to me. When I did go back inside, a gigantic, bespectacled Eraserhead baby was coming right at me.

"I don't want to talk about it."

I went out front and leaned on the counter. The screens overhead played *Risky Business*. I yanked the video out of the machine, dropped it on the floor, and crushed it with the heel of my sneaker. Carrie looked at me with her mouth open.

"That movie sucks."

Went over and looked right down into the counter where 30 episodes of the best of *Dark Shadows* from a really good source in upstate New York should be available for rent. Instead looking up at me were a bunch of comedies I let Evan stuff up there to make the place seem innocuous to any legal types snooping about. A few people started coming in, mostly to drop off returns and see if they were going to get their copy of *Nightmare on Elm Street*. I was handling the register when Lenny showed up. Once I could break free, the three of us were going back and forth about the *Dragon Lance* series. Both seemed to like it; not me. I butted in and asked if we could do the instant classic *Tomb of Horrors* by Gygax, and that just caught them dead. It was time to play the be all and end all of killer dungeons. No one gets out of this one alive boys, how fitting. I would run it once we finished *White Plume Mountains*. We got right down to about an hour of gaming, before it got too busy out front. Lenny split out the back door, sliding me a lifeline.

The rest of the day was nursed along with correct smoking. A couple of film fans asked me about the lack of stock, and I shrugged it off to a rush on rentals for the season. Evan left a bit early, all Brut by Fabareged up so any living creature within about six football fields away could smell him coming. He had that stupid tuxedo top on and walked out all full of his fucking self. Once he split I had a hard smoke. By the time I rolled through the Burger King drive-thru, I should not have been driving. I wanted to pull over or even go home, but that just was not going to happen. I ate while driving around some side streets; used to love Burger King cheese; something about that texture. And after the last bite went down the pipe and right to the bottom of my stomach, I was in her neighborhood again.

It was even colder than the night before, but people were everywhere. *Disorder* is the ambient sound, trying to dummy-up that skull sound hell-bent on breaking me. The lyrics were fading out and there she was sitting on a stoop on an abandoned triple decker. Everything froze right in its time stream, like it was Doctor Who or something. Yes. She does sit up.

Now what?

She is fumbling in her coat pocket for something. I gun it down the street, bang a U, and head back to her.

She sits up. So clear to me now. She sits up and probably spits in his face after she gets paid, but I've got to know. So much I *have to* know. Like are you the one who will bring me into the new age of pleasure? I find a space between two cars on the opposite side of the road and wrong-way park. Take a hard swig of my soda, draw two puffs out of a one-hitter, while watching her smoke. She flicks the first butt onto the ground and looks at the black sky for a minute. I try to open the door, but I am stuck in time while everything else passes me. After finishing the second cigarette she crushes it out with her foot and stands up.

"Don't go. Please don't go."

Everything sort of tightens inside me until she walks off down an alley and fades into nothingness. I grip the wheel as hard as I can, but it's useless. Go from freezing into place to a full force ejection. It really can't be getting this low, this fast, but it has. Walk-run-skip over there in a somnambulistic state and squat down with a small flashlight between my teeth. Rocks and glass numb sting my fingers as I sort through it all. I don't poke around anywhere there is a syringe.

Stand up from my scavenging just in time to see someone rummaging through my unlocked car. I start yelling and he takes off, just a figure really, carrying the bank envelope. Spin my wheels in all this debris beneath my feet, as he melts into shadows without making a sound. I run back to the car and take off. Can't call the cops. How could I explain being down in this shit-hole street now? They would think I got hoisted in a drug deal; what if the Chief found out? Drive around so much that I go from half a tank to gas light. *Gas Light*, another favorite of mine, and no doubt what I am doing to myself.

Evan was giving me the eye all morning, so I just stayed in my sections. To cool shit off, we had a chicken patty eating contest, ending tied at eight a-piece when we ran out of stock. Tried hard all morning not to vomit. Despite the large amount I had just dropped down, I felt okay and knew everything was going to work through me like it should. Just let it go, because she sits up. She does. She sits up.

The carpenters showed up to start work on the tanning room. This mustachioed Italian guy busted our balls a bit about how many chicks will be coming in to this place with nothing on but oil and bikinis. Evan and I somehow missed that angle, and that was a bit of something that I needed to swirl around in my thoughts. I was digging that vibe, until the dude said he would need a

$500 check by the end of the day. Evan wrote it out for him, and that is when everything started slipping.

I had about a grand in the bank, which would cover the losses, but really put a dent in my savings. Through all that static I began sorting through my options. I was replacing a copy of *CHUD* when it came to me. Kicked it all around for the rest of the day, and yet could not see a problem outside of maybe some surveillance cameras, and they can be tricked. My old man used to tell me gaming was a waste of time. That I should focus on getting back into school and make up for lost time; not pretending to be someone who actually did things. But gaming has taught me so much more than school ever could. What I had cooked up would prove it.

Everyone was getting ready to split for the night, and I would be left to take the envelope for deposit, since Evan was hot to move out and see this girl he wasn't saying anything about. He almost got by me, until I saw the top of the case sticking out from under his maroon Member's Only jacket.

"What video is that?"

"What video?"

Pointing right at it.

"*This?*"

"Yes *that.*"

He pulled out a copy of *Red Hatchet Murders.*

"You're gonna show your new girl that?"

"She said she loves these types of movies."

"And she likes you?"

"Fuck yeah."

"Best of luck man. You gotta bring her around here someday so I can talk film with her."

"Yeah, you never know."

He put on his headphones and hummed along to *Working Man* as he exited through the door. I locked up, then killed the lights out front, except for the sign. Took out the phone book and the receipt the Chief used to put down on the video camera. Called 411 and got a number for a money wiring service out in San Francisco; rang them up and had a cash order sent to the 24-hour supermarket near the edge of the town under the name of Ian Curtis. I drove home, which was on the way, and picked up a few things. At the strip mall, the only thing glowing neon was the supermarket sign. I passed by the darkened Zayres, City Bank, Thom McAn, Rexall, and parked in the front row. There were a few trucks pulling around back to unload freight, and at the other end of the lot a few vans were sporadically parked. Slid on the baseball cap, long rain coat with a woolen lining and some fake glasses from when I went as Peter Cushing for Halloween one year.

At the courtesy counter, where the wire service is located, stands a tall guy sporting round specs and a little blue knitted beany on top of his chrome dome. The lights here are so bright we both look pale as goddamned ghosts.

"Has a cash order for Mr. Ian Curtis arrived yet?"

He gives me the once over.

"Let me check, please."

He looks through this shoe box and takes out a slender slip of paper. A few decades ago I'd say this dude lost his love for this job.

"Can I see your ID please?"

"My ID?"

"Yes sir. A thing with your name and address and even a real photo of you on it."

"I don't have one on me."

"I'm not supposed to give out any orders to someone who doesn't have an ID."

"Look man, I need to get this cash to the hospital, because they won't see my dad because he has no insurance."

"What's wrong with him?"

"They don't know, I think."

"Really?"

"It's bad man."

He looks at the slip and says: "One thousand dollars is a lot of money."

"Sure is. All we've got in the world."

"So... if it is yours, why was it wired here?"

"Long story, you know."

"Even ten percent of that is a lot."

He lays out the cash until there are ten even piles of twenties, scoops one of the stacks towards himself, and nods at the others. I grab my share and split. My luck held since I charged more than I really needed. Felt it was only right to use some of his cash to buy weed. One way or the other I was getting some sort of payback, no matter how small.

Heart racing as I head for the door. I'm about to turn out of aisle when my new best friend calls my attention. Everything inside me wants to scatter.

I turn to him more than I should.

"Yeah?"

"Ian lives."

"Right on."

Won that one too. If I had said my name was Robert Plant, that guy would have never let me pass.

Drove back to the store, got an envelope from the file cabinet and walked it down to the bank. Back in the store, with the lights off, things started going south in my head, like with the music and her voice from the tape which wasn't quite in time with the music. I was so tired I knew there was no way I could ever sleep. Picked up some Burger King and drove home. Ate everything in the car while sitting in the driveway. My dad's bedroom light was on, cut into uneven sections by the branch of this old tree. I remember in high school we read *To Kill a Mockingbird* by Truman Capote. There was this old tree this albino dude used to put stuff in for these little kids as signs of friendship. I always pictured it was that tree when I read the thing. There is no hole in my tree though. Sat out there until the light went off in dad's bedroom, then I went up to my place.

Back in my room, staring at Debbie Harry's stretched and wave-lengthed lips, hoping sleep would come to me, feeling quite satisfied at what I had done. Tonight I wouldn't watch a video. Tonight I would think of it myself and really concentrate. Tonight I can make it as close to something real with someone real as you can get. And I try. But there is no actual feeling-nothing to touch; there never is, and there never has been. But there is something that seems even lonelier tonight than failing to feel anything; the thought of using the screen yet again. Through the dark that motherfucker can cut you into smashed glass pieces. Yet I can't live without her. It's the only thing that keeps the doors to my own personal theatre locked. It is really late, or maybe really early, when

I quit trying to fool myself and pull the tape. With my back to the screen I do what I have to do, listening just to her calling him those awful names. Even this is no longer any good.

When I wake up the next morning I am face down atop the three big tubs of my videos. No idea how they got out here. A cruel mirror reveals I have a small shiner under my right eye. Fill the sink up and stick my face into the cold water like that fucking Huey Lewis video Carrie loves so much. Spots passing by my eyes as my lips turn numb.

"Why?"

"You take care of getting films that people like in here. That's your part. I'll take care of the money. I want to show my old man that I can do these things, you know?"

Wendy's late one night in the middle of winter, a pisser of a freezing day. There we are having Frosties. *Every Breath You Take,* is playing in the place, bugging the shit out of me. Evan is having his own cunty time, and we are dead on serious about getting this going.

"I mean if you want to."

"I got some good ideas."

Evan can see what his life is becoming if he keeps going down his current path. He has started law school at Suffolk University after graduating from Rutgers. I used to go down on the bus and visit him once and a while. Every time I went to this tiny apartment he had with two other guys, he was either drunk or stoned, or really depressed because he just could no longer study the law. He hated it that much. Evan never told me what the old man said when the prodigal son returned home with a 0.6 GPA and was told not to return to school.

His dad has been stiff-arming him into clerking or some shit down at the family law firm. That is some serious drudgery. And I am slowly dying as well; constantly tired, losing weight, coughing all the time, and probably have an ulcer, all from working in a fucking mill. My job was cutting these huge rolls of carpet, which fucking stink, and having lunch with people who, literally, can barely read. I looked around at myself and said, "This is where I've landed."

That's when I called the pow-wow. We will no longer be prisoners. I already have the money saved for my half of the investment. Evan is a little short still, since he is forever blowing tons of cash on women to get them to look at him. It's as far as he gets. Evan's dad actually ends up helping him a little bit, but I know the real reason. He wants us to fail. Then Evan will have to crawl back to him for money to go back to law school, and be humbled like he just met the Iron Sheik. Then, when he's suffered just enough, he'll be given a nice job and start paying this old man back for the loan he gave us to start our beloved Metropolitan Video.

Gradually, Evan would creep his way onto the movie part of the biz, but I knew he would. It's not a terrible idea because a lot of our customers love the same vanilla, Hollywood tripe that he does. I wouldn't have a Spielberg film in here outside of *Jaws*, which is amazing, if it were up to me. But his real strength is mingling with the masses and dealing with our cash. He even calls the bank every, *every*, business day at one to make sure the nightly deposit went through. He even slaps on this stupid green visor with a white $ on it I got him for his birthday last year. I saw the thing in Woolworths for a buck. He does get the joke, but still...

I was out stocking shelves when he found me and said: "What the hell happened to you?"

"Walked into a door. It was sideways, you know?"

"How did you fuck up your lip on the left side and eye on the right?"

"I dunno."

"Anyways," slowly, "guess what?" with a big smile.

"What?"

"We actually made more money than I thought yesterday. I had recorded seven hundred eleven, and the cash was actually seven sixty. More grub I say!"

"In*deed*!"

Evan took off for the food and I walked around my sections to decompress. I'd covered my tracks, fucked the Chief over, and there was no way anyone could ever pin anything on me. I put *Polyester* on the screens and got to work cleaning anywhere that needed it, especially around the new room, where there was a sawdust trail. Inside the chamber lays a strange and alien sarcophagus. The lighting is dim and a strange hum emanates from the tomb. Through the double half doors, the smell becomes more and more grease laden. The lighting is poor, but the colors shoot at you like a glossy haze. You make your saving throw and move back to where the treasure is. Wandering monsters! Three troglodytes enter the main room and are prowling around.

Caller: "I just watch."

It takes them a few minutes to find the lichen and moss they have been searching for: *Arthur, Grease II, American Anthem, Nobody's Perfekt,* and *Mommy Dearest.* They give me their gold and I make my charisma roll. Everyone gets what they want.

Evan came back and we immediately heated up two of the *Hungry Men Salisbury Steak* meals he snagged. Carrie and Larry, a laid off teacher we employ part time, were busy with the registers, so it was peaceful, and we locked ourselves in the back room. As the cooking ceremony was ticking off, we got out the pipe and headed to the alley, where we whacked it around and good. When the bell rang, we got down to it. No one said a word until at least one of their steaks was gone.

"Did your girl like *Deep Red?*"

"She loved it. I want to get her a copy."

"Wow, it's that serious, huh?"

"She's wicked awesome, man."

"How old?"

"Our age."

"A lot of the copies, even ours, has about thirteen minutes missing. Some have almost a half an hour missing."

There is this unique texture to Salisbury Steak that I love.

"Plus, you know, that tape ain't gonna be cheap. Fifty maybe. We can get it from the distributor almost wholesale."

"I don't care."

"I could dupe it for her. I'd make it look tit."

"No. I gotta get her one in the box."

"Don't tell me you appreciate the box art now."

"I don't. Just a box to me. But she does."

"This one might just might be a keeper. She's not going back to Israel, is she?"

He just gets this big fuck-you grin on his face while he slides two fried chicken dinners into the nuker. There was something comforting about the smell of the chicken. My mother used to heat them up in the ovens. I also like Libby Land, but those are more for a snack. We ate in relative peace, talking mostly about strategy to survive *S2: Caverns of Tsojacanth*. You need to go very slowly and open only one door a day. That will give you time to recover. Half the fun, is actually getting there. We lost O'Naris the Magic User to a blast of lightning from a Blue Dragon before we even got near the place.

Lenny came around and we slid in a good 90 minutes of gaming. Carrie manned the till, and Larry stocked and did whatever else. The game put me in good head. To keep me from sinking, I kept *Polyester* running on a loop. Tab Hunter not receiving every award possible for his performance here is a crime. He was never better; very few ever were that great. David Samson is pretty amazing as well. It's one of the funnier John Waters movies you can show to the public without the cops being called. Today they were coming in steadily, and we had the popcorn machine firing away and the place smelled great. People were laughing out loud at some of the scenes on the screens–especially the "crazy honky" part. I once owned three Odorama cards. One is kept in the store's glass counter, on full display with a sign saying: "Yup, it's real!"

At nine I let Larry go home after paying him in cash. Then Carrie and I cleaned up the place as Evan brought the deposit down to the bank. He took off from there. Paid Carrie in cash as well, and she headed out to who knows where, saying she was off to buy a carton of cigarettes first. I dropped the blinds over the front windows and vacuumed the floor again, watching the movie again on the overheads. Nuked two pizzas and downed them with a 2-litre of Mountain Dew. Checked out the street through the slats in the blinds, got my bag out of the ceiling, then sat on the futon and rolled a tight one. About half way through the paper started really getting black and were slowing and all is very peaceful. I carefully put it out on the bottom on my sneaker, then just started walking around the place.

I turned V66 on the TVs, but the VJs were getting to me, and then they went to play *Billie Don't Lose That Number*, so off it went. Got the boom box out and cued up *Turn It On Again* by Genesis off of this mix-tape I made. It took me about thirty minutes of listening to that song again and again, to get the place looking really tops.

Then what? I knew what it would take, so I went back and smoked the rest of the joint. I was now in no condition to drive and Rule Number One is, "You shall not endanger anyone or anything while experiencing the Tree of Life." This old Hippie dealer we had when we were like 14 used to tell us that. He wouldn't even let us buy if we rode our bikes. He's now in the Tree in the Sky.

With my eyes bleeding I go through the saloon doors and find copies of *Insatiable* and *Talk Dirty to Me Part III*. Ghosts of 1,000 lonely hand jobs swirl around me. They stink of hand creme and desperation. These white apparitions pay me no mind; they're all as lonely as I am. Shot-gun three Millers and take a hard piss. Then out comes the store brand creme, and off go the fluorescent tubes and on the screen they come.

But look at these people; have they found what they wanted here? Will I? How do I even get there? And when I do will I be so debased that getting rammed up the ass by someone dressed as Madonna, calling me a faggot every five seconds, will be the only thing left for me? That next step is impossible to avoid, isn't it? And the naked bodies on the screen right now writhing and sweating while their moans are obviously overdubbed and these fairly new tapes are already wearing out in certain places. It's just mouths and eyes and cunts, gaping clean assholes and it is all too much, wrapping all around me, with pixilated tentacles, dragging me into them, merging, there is no more me, I am an image now and nothing more, ephemeral mixing amongst these others trapped in time.

Woke up on the futon with a mild headache and baboon pussy breath. I showered and got into some clean clothing: a pair of khakis and a t-shirt reading VIDEODROME HAS AN AGENDA. I was so taken by that masterpiece that I had this hand pressed at the mall after seeing it for the third time in one day. The idiots were revolted and completely confused by this film's genius that day. Those pussies walked out before Debbie Harry takes off her clothes. Not me. I knew what it was all about. I am a child of the VCR and the constant luster of The New Flesh. To me that movie is a harbinger about life to come.

I retrieved the returns, rewound the tapes that needed it, wrote down fines, and shelved the boxes. How hard is it to rewind? We have three re-winders here we got from Zayers for ten bucks each. It's the easiest thing; push a goddamn button. Yet they bitch when they get fined. I show them the little yellow and black sticker with the bee on it, and they begrudgingly slap over the buck. I had the place spotless and was about to pick a movie to play when Evan came in holding a tape and whistling *There is Something About You*, so off-key that only a Geddy Lee fan could appreciate it.

"Sup Hanks?"

"Nothing Baumgartner."

"I just heard some Level 42 on the radio. Pretty good stuff. But I gotta hear some Rush, and *now*."

"Put on your headphones man. Seriously. If I hear *Subdivisions* one more fucking time, I will puke on your fuckin' forty-dollar shirt."

"You got no taste."

"*I* got no taste?"

"No, you don't. Look at that cheesy shirt you're wearing."

"*This shirt?* You *are* an idiot."

"That shirt wouldn't have worked in 1976, you know that?"

The I see an opening.

"What tape is that there?" pointing to one tucked away in his maroon Members Only jacket.

"What do you care? It's a return."

"No it's not. I cleared out all the returns. Now let's see it."

"Eat me."

"It will prove my theory of your taste."

"I don't care."

"Yes you do."

"I *don't.*"

"Let me see that tape, man."

"Suck my ass."

He's sorts puffed out at me, but I don't budge. I'm no big guy, and Evan is three inches taller than me, but weighs ten pounds less and those glasses don't send fear into anyone's heart. He should be behind a Dungeon Master's screen until his age catches up with his face. And the puffy baby blue tuxedo top with the black bow tie he is wearing isn't really doing much more than making me crack up.

"C'mon man. Let's see. Prove me wrong."

He turns it over like he's Vanna fucking White. *New Wave Hookers.*

"I thought you were going out with that girl last night?"

"I did."

"You go back to her place?"

"Yeah."

"*And?*" pointing at the tape.

"Well, yeah, you know."

He smuggled the thing out right under my nose last night. What a move.

"You still listen to Rush," walking off.

Emptiness met me around the corner and had be in pieces before I knew what was what. Everything is changing so quickly, and I am crazy and getting crazier. Something had to happen. I begged the Universe to send me something, a sign, a quick death, anything. And right after lunch, with the electrician making noise like all hell while hooking up the cancer bed, there was a response. Tight jeans, white top, real firm cans and I could smell that flesh-sweetness when she walked by the counter without noticing me. Ogled her without being caught the whole time she was there. At the counter, she gave me her rental: *Staying Alive*.

"Have you seen *Saturday Night Fever?*"

"No," she said.

"It's much better than this."

"O."

No one is perfect, but still you need to have a baseline standard, even if you do like Caren Kaye with a not so great bleach job. It all went cold for me until she handed me the pen back after signing the rental agreement. Our finger tips touched. That's all it took of the real thing to start it all up again. Played it cool until she left, then bolted for the can and took care of business. Ten pumps for every turn of the screw. No use for shampoo; over before it really began. For a while I sat on the can pants down, panting, sweating and maybe crying with my dick dripping into the water. That simple touch had awoken something else inside me. Something that for so long I had tried to deny myself. Something that was almost as terrifying as the darkness creeping about in my head. But now I was charged and the moon was full, and all sorts of thoughts were charging through me. Around 4 p.m. I took a quick walk down to the corner and bought an alternative paper from a machine, hustling it back under my sweatshirt.

Slid *The Wolfman* into our floor top-loader and it broke that blackness, burning right out of both screens. I manned the front counter and when no one was around looked at the ads at the back of the tabloid. Some of the ink was coming off in my hands. I took the thing into the can with the cordless. Two gave me the run around, and I backed off quickly. The third one *Ladies Only* was super professional and asked me all these questions about what I would really like: height, hair, lips, tits ass shaved or unshaved clean or unclean tall or short and even the eyes. Even though I would pay cash, they needed a credit card as a deposit. If I paid in person, it wouldn't show up on the bill. I used the Chief's number again without fear of being caught, then reserved a room at the 495 Holiday Inn off Exit 50C with it.

Why I decided to torture myself with *The Wolfman*, I don't know. It was really getting to me, the parts where he wants to be tied up before the sun goes down and the part where he does this weird shit to meet a girl across town. For him it works. Yet I kept my eyes right onto the screens the whole time. Carrie kept talking to me about the movie, which helped me remain in light, simply because I had to block out her comments.

"Shouldn't he have a longer snout?... I wouldn't want someone to look at me through a telescope. That's fucking creepy." And not surprisingly: "That was maybe the best black and white movie I've ever seen." That's the thing, it's not that she hates great movies, it's that she also loves the *most wretched* films, and in a way, that's worse, because she has absolutely *no* art filter whatsoever. Being around her, and that weird longing for what I hadn't cashed in on, made the day even crueler. Inside I was burning, wondering what would it be like tonight. Kept a decent high on most of the afternoon, as the night lay ahead full of stomach churning wonder.

The tanning booth and room were now ready. It's first victim was Carrie who used it for over an hour, coming out color of the Hamburglar. Watching her walk all around in a white bikini, sheening and shining with sweat had me revved up all the way up past the top, and I had to date the shampoo again, even if her skin color was fucked. All signs were pointing to something big happening tonight. Someone will actually touch me tonight. They will have no choice; I am paying for it.

When Evan and Carrie left, I just wanted to fucking die, pacing all over the place trying to psyche myself up. Wet and combed my Moe Howard twenty times in the mirror and finally sprayed it into place. Then it was me and fluorescent lights and out of nowhere, like that scene in *Jaws* when the shark is coming at you, but it's too blurry to quite make it out, but you sure as fuck know what it is, something was closing in. The fin is about to rise out of the depths and breach this dark glass surface. I am now terrified and nowhere near the shore.

The eight-track is playing *Disorder* as I pull into the parking lot of the hotel. Sit there eating McNugget after McNugget; washing it down with two large Cokes. I couldn't taste a thing. From under the passenger seat I pulled the 40 of Heffenreffer I picked up at the Korean market on my way here, and guzzled half of it nonstop. It took two more pulls to kill the thing. I chucked the bottle into the back seat, Then took my stuff out of my trunk and went inside with me head down. At the desk-One of my former customers-She's a dish and a half with red hair, but also the one I got into it with.

"Hi, I just saw you while driving by and thought I would stop in and say hi." Trying to figure something out.

"You ready to tell me?"

"I'll say this, come back to the store and we will talk. You were a great customer."

"Not until you say it."

"Maybe another time."

"What's with all the stuff?"

"This stuff? Just didn't want to leave it in the car while I said hello. But I gotta rock. Love the blazer."

Split as fast as I can and hit 495 south driving so as not to draw attention. My confidence is rising since I handled that potential disaster adroitly and without looking like I was up to something. Getting pretty good at this. What the fuck are the odds she would be at that place? What are the odds, because I will gladly put a dollar down on that? My hands are shaking. She was not at the desk when I reserved the room this afternoon, it was some dude. Take an off ramp and pull into a motel village I've seen off the highway a million times. There are ten cottages, and three have cars in front of them; one being a pretty sharp red Corvette. The gravel driveway is blanketed with cigarette butts, one at the front door still burning near its filter.

Inside it reeks even more of cigarettes, but stack that on top of piss, and that's close enough. At the counter, half nodded out, is this total GG Allin fan, wearing a vest, jean cutoffs, and no shirt, smoke blowing out his mouth on every breath. Somehow he manages to take $30 from me, hand me a key, and mumble something about cottage ten. I use the payphone outside in front of the office. A cop car passes in the far above us on the highway with its lights flashing. I call *Ladies Only* and let them know where I am. It is closing in on 11 and I apologize for calling so late, but they didn't get too worked up about it. This bungalow, which looks like one of those prebuilt sheds you can buy at Grossman's is set back near some woods which run up a hill. Directly behind my cottage is a steaming swamp. You can just see the Shambling Mounds and Ropers ready to grab your ass.

Caller: Weapons and spells at the ready, everyone.

Inside the cabin there is a twin bed, table with two chairs and a port-a-john connected to it by this makeshift bi-fold door. Oddly enough it doesn't smell all that terribly. Sort of like when you throw some Pine Sol around to cover the smell lingering from the vacuum. There is a double socket light in the middle of the ceiling. Stand on the bed and replace it with two bulbs that I brought. Open my case, and set up the equipment. It takes me about fifteen minutes, and the whole time I hum *Photograph* by Def Leppard. Total chick band, but that's a pretty good pop rock song. After that I don't even bother to put a towel under the door; just light up right near the shithouse. The smoke slowly finds the cracks between the rooms. I fuck around with the positioning of the lights, hoping the girl will have maybe an Ally Sheedy look.

She knocks at one minute to midnight, and being this high keeps me from puking. Steady myself and open the door. About five seven, little shorter than me, wearing blue neon stretch pants and a red half shirt, she fills things out a little more than I like, and her face is nothing for the screen, but it is good enough in a slut way. She is nothing like I ordered.

"C'mon in. I'm sorry about this place. The hotel desk clerk at the nice hotel knew me. What could I do?"

"It's okay."

Her eyes run all over me, then the room.

"Why don't you check under the bed and all over 'til you feel comfortable." I fold open the door exposing an empty can.

"What's with the camera?"

"I, well look, I want to film this."

"O, listen..." taking a step back. "That will cost you a lot."

"How much?"

She does some phantom calculation in her head. "Five hundred."

"This is my first time, you know?"

"*Is it?*" kinda sarcastic.

"Yes."

"I've been many guys' first."

"Do I get a first timers discount?"

She chuckles a little and lights a cigarette. Someone outside screams something at something. Nothing screams back.

"Only frequent flyer discounts."

"What's your name?"

"What is my name tonight for this film?"

"I don't know. I mean, Mira cool?"

"Sure."

I had switched the money from the deposit envelope to my left front pocket. I pull it out and give her what she wants.

"And my performance fee?"

Shell out the five hundred in all sorts of bills. She takes it as soon as it appears, stuffing it into her white glitter purse.

"Now you don't have to worry about this going on your credit card. And then there is my tip."

"I'm paying you half a grand extra as it is."

"I know baby, and guess what, I am going to make it super special for you. Tonight, I am the only one for you, right? That's worth it, trust me."

"How old are you Mira?"

"Old as you need me to be."

"You wanna get high first?"

Thin, carefully painted eyebrow raises just a bit: "What ya got?"

She seems a bit disappointed that it is weed, but we smoke it up just the same. It's killer, so there are no complaints.

"Can I give you some weed as a tip?"

"I've got to make so much money every night before I can turn a profit. So I can only take cash. Now coke..."

"Yeah, sorry."

"Okay, let's get going."

Walk over to my setup and power it all up. The on light burns red-eye at me from the camera. I am mostly concerned about the focus, because we are about to go live. My chest is burning and burning burning burning with like this acidic lightning. Much more intense than when Carrie came at me; much more distant as well. Mira stands up and crushes her smoke out into the silver McDonalds ashtray on the table.

"Okay, what would you like?"

Her eyes are torched up red from the lights and she's even got a crimson tint to her face. A little succubus come to not drain me of my soul, but to give me one. My best Cleric ever might not be able to turn her. She is reeking her musk and trying to Charm you all the same. Saving throw. Might be dying. She pulls down those suspenders around her waist and yanks off her top; pretty nice rack, although it is already heading south a bit, and there are some ski slopes developing. Down goes the rest of it. It's right there in front of me. But how many guys have fucked that? What the hell is swimming around in there, just waiting to give me something. And then there is what if I can't do it. What then? More humiliation. There is something awful about the droopy look of her cunt. Pull that dead skin back and there is a mouth full off needles just waiting to tear me apart, body and soul. I undress slowly. She see's what I am looking at, and does the worst thing possible by opening it up and showing me that evil eye; the one that watches. All hell, Orcus, Jubliex, King of Flies, they're all laughing in my face. Saving throw is a critical miss. By the time I am down to my briefs, she senses the trouble. Soon it hangs there like a dead rat, all for the camera to record.

She gets on her knees and comes at it with her hands behind her back. Her fingers are folded up, forming a dorsal fin. Those dead black eyes stay open as she lets that mouth full of ten thousand teeth start to do its best. It's got a little life, but now my eyes are fixed on that red light. Try my best to picture it on a dirty screen in some 42nd Street shit hole at 2 in the morning, with all the winos sitting around you, just looking to be ripped off. But all your eyes focus on is this chump not able to get his dick hard. He's almost hyperventilating when she says to him: "Maybe if you turn the camera off, you will be able to focus a bit more."

"Not the camera?" eyes wide.

"Really?" it still hangs next to her face.

"I want to be able to watch this forever and ever."

"Just close your eyes and think of whoever you want me to be."

We both want this to be over.

She moves in and takes the thing all the way down her throat, where it slogs along. Pick up her vibe and start to play my part. She is the bitch and I am the stud and together we will make some sort of ever-lasting magnetic bastard child. This is forever and it doesn't matter if it is real now does it? And then she gets on top, grinding away on my sluggish worm until she works up to the fake orgasm. Then there is the slide down and more deep throating, pretending to swallow my load; even wipes her mouth looking straight into the camera.

"A star is born."

Evan didn't waste any time letting me know how terrible I looked and even was kind enough to mention how bad I smelled.

"How many days in a row have you worn that Moving Pictures t-shirt under your little blouse there?"

"I *wash* the thing."

"For your info, they were flushing the hydrants on my street and I didn't want to bathe in rust. Is that okay with you?"

"Well at least clean up."

"Thanks for the advice, *faggot*."

"You're the one who smells like an ass-faggot."

I showered and took a few puffs to make me forget some stuff. Didn't help, but what it did do was open me up to a new idea. What if I could do that again, but watch the first movie we made while doing it? That might be just the thing to help me turn the corner and finally get the job done. Even if we did have to go that motel again, I could bring a TV and VCR and let it rip... There's a jump in my reel and now I am hanging up the phone after speaking with a very polite woman at *Ladies Only*.

Carrie was working the register, again complimenting someone on a terrible movie choice: *Zapped!* with Scott Fucking Baio and Willie Aimes. How can someone with her raw level of intelligence could enjoy a movie like that? It does have the amazing duo of Lawanda Page and Scatman Crother's, but that wasn't where Carrie was coming from. That really stuck with me until Lenny came by with some good stuff and we kicked off *Tomb of Horrors*. I was DMing this instant legend of a module, and both of them rolled up two characters worth 30 levels total. Numb nuts numbers geek Evan tried to make a level one Magic User and then a 29th level Cleric. Had to call bullshit on that, and he went on and on. I finally had to cap it on nothing lower than 12th level. I mean an 18th level MU gets one ninth level spell, which includes the Death Spell or Wish. He finally relented and played an 18th level cleric and 12th level dwarven fighter, bitching the whole fucking time about how I wrecked his plan. Lenny played human twins–one a fighter and one a thief, both 15th level. Only a fool brings their own character to this one.

They had just discovered the correct entrance, when Lenny had to split back to his office. I guess around 3 p.m. they do a head count or something. Evan and I took back our store, and started shelving the afternoon returns. It is best after an intense gaming session to do something right away, instead of staying in that dimension. Try to time it so I start out stoned, and by the time the game is over I am sober and back to what I guess is reality. I know when I am there, because the nausea starts up again.

Worked the register for a while, watching the street outside turn dark and the headlights moving by, dulled a little bit through a moving silver mist. Yuppies are always in the lot where I park, sitting in their Beamers, constantly looking everywhere, snorting cocaine off the edges of credit cards or keys. They're all getting numbed up to head home to the suburbs and the lives they hate so fucking much. Why else would you have to get so whacked? Watching all those heads going up and down shoved right into my face that the night was here now, and soon I would have to go out into it again. Maybe I shouldn't. Maybe I should just have everything happen here. Too dangerous if someone sees something. Do I want someone like that coming here and knowing who I really am? What I really am? The new flesh desperate to be made whole. That made me even edgier and more isolated, because if I didn't complete what I had to do, there would be no one who could reach me. And then what? Tonight, I knew, I had to be a man-for the first time be a fucking man, and save myself.

It was my night to drop off the envelope. Before coming into my store today, I stopped by the bank and took out the cash from my own account to cover the night before. It was only right. I would try and pull another wire scam in a few days to make up for it. If that same guy is there, it will cost, but the Chief will be the one who ends up stuck with the bill. I paced, drank a few wine coolers, then watched some tapes I'd made of *Night Flight*. The noise in my head was cutting straight through me. Smoked three quarters of a bone and things seemed to slow up just enough. Before leaving, I called the hotel again and she answered. I hung up right away.

"Fuck."

Went out and got my car, parking it in the alley facing head out. I took one of the two overhead TVs and brought it down from its bracketing and placed it in my trunk along with the camera and bulbs that were needed. I stopped off first for some drive-thru, then drove slowly to the cottages. There were five motorcycles, all Harleys, parked in front of one of the shacks closest to the road.

Another cabin had the same red Corvette parked in front of it. GG Allin's biggest fan was working the desk, and gave me the same place as before. I parked about thirty feet away and carried my gear inside. The bikers were running train on some poor bitch who was screaming in either sheer pain or sheer delight. It was impossible for me to tell.

After setting everything up, I called *Ladies Only* from the outside phone. One of the bikers was wearing nothing but a vest, sitting in front of his door, smoking a cigarette and jerking his hog in a somnambulistic state. The noises and sounds have not changed. He doesn't seem to notice me hot-footing back. By the time she shows up everything is in place, and I am rock hard from watching the video three times. It is a new girl, and right away the vibe goes bad.

"Who are you?"

"I'm Joelle."

"That was the name of that dead girl, wasn't it?"

She stops cold for a second to look at me. Continuing in: "Is that what you want?"

"No. No. No. Come in I guess."

"What's with all this shit?"

"I want to film this. You know?"

"Then what is that on the TV over there?" her face scrunches up; not scared, but she knows this is a bit weird, even for this place.

"Trick photography."

"Okay... You have my money?"

Hand her the two hundred. She counts it in front of me, nods and gives me a weak smile. This one has had a lot of life sucked out of her, and her face shows every place it was pulled from. Her left cheek isn't quite right. Betting it was crushed in then rebuilt. She takes the cash and puts it into one of those fuzzy pocket books, then takes off her long leather coat. It is red garters and the Ginger Lynn style lingerie. She's sporting smoky colored nylons to cover up some obvious spider webs.

"Okay, well, it is extra for the filming."

"How much?"

"Okay, you give me eighty bucks. I make a call, and then a guy shows up, I get feeling good and then I really won't care."

"Okay."

She throws her coat on and goes out to the pay phone. You can hear that the biker party getting really freaky. This is freaking me out. She runs back after making the call, and closes the door.

"That's some fucked up shit going on out there. Priests of Judah biker gang. All meth freaks. Crazy fucking people. Never fuck with them."

"Do you know the Chief?"

"Who?"

"The Chief. Do you know the Chief?"

"I have no idea what you are talking about."

"Cause if you are, this is entrapment."

She slides her jaw across those cigarette yellow teeth for a moment.

"That really doesn't hold up in court, you know?"

"So do you know the Chief?"

"No. I do not. And I am not a cop. Plus the money you gave me is for my travelling expenses to here only."

"So you don't know the Chief?"

"*No.* I do not know the Chief? Who? The Chief of police?"

"Yes."

"He's one person I don't want to know."

"Why?

"*Cause he's a cop.* I don't know him, okay?"

I think it over for a minute and come up with another test. She paces the room.

"You wanna get high?"

She takes out a metal pipe and I put some weed into the bowl. She starts to smoke.

"I've got a little cold sore. Don't worry though, you can't get it on your cock. And you can't kiss me, so..."

"Okay."

We sit there stoned and I am staring straight at that cold sore rising from under the lipstick, ready to pop and fester.

Cars approach in the driveway

"This is my man."

She opens the door, takes one step out, and we both can see them closing right in, blue and white light spinning through the darkness. Fourth, fifth then a sixth cruiser comes racing in, lights on. A bunch of Staties are pounding on the door of the biker's cabin. One of the cops has some sort of hand cannon, dropping a canister down the barrel.

"Run!" Joelle screams.

Next thing I know I am high tailing it into the woods and up a hill as the door on the biker's cabin is blown open. Two cops are yelling for us to stop. Keep hauling. They follow with flashlights, closing in on our heels. I lose them up the hill, reaching a small underpass beneath the highway. Remain squatting down in there, listening to this deafening traffic which is mainly large trucks manned by over-methed drivers. Everything around me shakes and vibrates with hate. No idea where the girl has vanished; it's everyone for themselves right now. I am wearing my calculator watch, and the minutes come and go for two hours. Then there is a voice in my head reminding me of what is inside that cabin. Move slowly down the wet hills, steam rising up, and there are wandering monsters everywhere. Kneel behind a tree about fifty feet from the cabin and watch the cleanup. Everything is strewn about from several cabins and the lights are still on in the main hut. Once the scene is clear, I go down to my cabin.

Sit on the concrete slab of a stoop and light up.

The sun will be up soon, and I am about six miles from home.

A half an hour before Evan was due, I called my car and equipment in as stolen. Even if the Chief did hear about this, what would he care? Motherfucker would probably find it a riot. I did not call the insurance company. All I needed was for that fucking dick to come snooping around. All for the fucking pursuit of happiness I would be crucified. My hope was that all my shit was in a lot somewhere and I could go get it. A cop I had never seen showed up alongside the bug-eyed Evan.

"Someone stole my car from right out of the alley."

"*What?*"

"Discovered it about a half an hour ago."

The cop was an okay guy who took down all the info with professional boredom. I could feel Evan about to explode when he heard what stuff had been in the trunk. It took about fifteen minutes, and the cop left saying: "Sorry about your loss. We will do what we can do. But make sure you let your insurance company know."

Evan looked me up and down, then let it out.

"*Back*!" pointing to the door with his thumb.

It was the first time I ever let anyone talk to me like that in my own store, but I fucked up and had to take this. It was only right. Inside he starts ranting, asking me about what the camera was doing out?

"I was using it."

"There's a three month wait and you were using one? I hope you were making some money for us."

I said nothing.

"So what is going on with you?"

"Nothing."

"Things don't add up."

Stomach's now flooding with acid.

"What do you mean?"

"Like when you got busted going to do returns on Joelle Caldwell."

"What about it?"

"I wanted to see what movies they still had so I could take them off our system. They never had an account here."

I thought of the old, well someone lent the tapes to them, but he'd see right through it.

"Are you practicing for law school?"

"No, I'm wondering what the hell is up with you? You're like out of your mind lately. What's going on?"

"Nothing."

"Bullshit."

"Just all this shit with the Chief put me off. You know, I kept the camera in the car because I had it on record. I wanted to see if he would come near my car."

"On some random night?"

"No. It was more that we got a return and I kept it. I'm sorry. I'll pay for the night's rental."

"And the fucking TV? What's up with that?"

"Tube blew."

"Bullshit." Looking way down his glasses at me. "Everything you've said to me is bullshit."

"Look, I gotta get to the insurance company," turning tail and running out the back door.

I had no intention of going to that place. The plate was now called in as stolen and soon it would turn up in their system, and I'd have to go to an impound lot somewhere. I went to the bank, withdrew the rest of my life's savings, and replaced the money that I again had lost for the store. Shoved all those hard fought bills into a blue leather envelope and slid it into the slot on the side of the bank. My hope was the real deposit rested safely in the trunk, where I stashed it beneath the spare tire.

Walked a few blocks trying to come up with something, but it was brick wall after brick wall. I went to the Korean market and bought a 40 ounce of Budweiser, and drank it all in the alley, sitting on some milk crates. Maybe the owner will come out and enlighten me with some ancient wisdom. The only thing that happens is a dog walks by the alley, barely looking my way. Started back with my hands in my pockets. There were signs of support for the Patriots in all these windows. Guess they were the rage that year. It meant nothing to me.

When I got back to the store, Evan had already taken a call from the cops. I rang back without thinking, and they said my car was in an impound lot near the motel. I caught a break after the fiasco last night when someone who worked at one of the Wendy's I always go to drove by me on the highway and stopped. He brought me to my store on the way to his work, never asking what I was doing out there. I hung up, went out to the back, got my bike, and pedaled out to the lot.

This was a real place of misery. There were two trailers and tons of fence topped off with rusty barbed wire. Shitty car after shitty car after dented car after totaled car filling this big rock and dirt lot that's totally coated by butts. There was even some dog barking and growling from someplace; the sound was everywhere, maybe even piped in. Three greasy tow trucks blocked the openings, which were already double pad locked. I had to go into Trailer A, which was for stolen vehicles. This abomination of the funhouse fat woman sporting this year's version of the Bride of Frankenstein hairdo and the newest Divine-style makeup, called me over. I show her my ID and there is some paper work to fill out. Then she calls someone and in a minute this real weedy looking runt comes in with a Morning in America t-shirt and pants made solely of grease.

"O. That one is yours? Yeah, well, you can't drive it out of here."

"Why?"

"Busted windshield. You can't drive it."

"They broke my windshield?"

"Guess so."

"So what do I do?"

"Well you just call your insurance company and they will fix it for free. But I don't want them to do it here. This is my space, not theirs like they think it is. I'll tow it somewhere for you."

I give him my store's address.

"Twenty bucks."

In my pocket rested $46.64 cents which was everything left over.

"Fine."

He drives my car out to the front and I immediately open the trunk. Pull up the tire and find nothing there. The motherfuckers cleaned me out. I dropped my bike in, closed it up, and slid in next to the driver in the truck. He starts to tell me about his back surgery. I talk right over him and ask about where I can get someone to put in a windshield for cash. He knows about ten people, and hands me the oiliest cards imaginable for two of them. He parks my ride face in to the alley, since I had no intention of spending my own cash to fix the glass. I paid the troll and off he went without saying anything. Slid inside my ride and looked everywhere trying to find anything, but the vultures had picked me clean. They would also have the tapes and the cameras. No doubt the Staties will eye them, and maybe the Chief finds out then. No way they give me back my stuff. Either way I can't do shit about it. That's the feeling that makes you do just about anything.

Lenny was in the back with Evan; Carrie and Larry in the front. The two were just about to smoke and

I joined right in. They were both looking at me funny. Doubt Evan would have told Lenny about his suspicions, but these were strange end days. I got behind the screen and ran two more hours of *The Tomb of Horrors,* like nothing had just happened. They had made it down the first hall, not too worse for the wear, and had arrived at the Great Hall of Spheres. Lenny as the thief was hitting rolls like you cannot believe, and a few Detract Traps spells helped a lot. Evan was pushing the tempo, and I could tell Lenny was getting pissed. We had talked about playing this for years, yet here it is and Baumgartner is just looking around for something to hack up. But then the later day customer rush was starting, and it was nearing head count time for Len, so we called it, and went back to business. One thing I wanted to get done before it all came tumbling down was finishing playing this module.

It was getting a bit later into the afternoon and the sun was working its way down, making everything outside haze October orange. Events were going on right now concerning me. I could feel him, cold and alien, those black eyes locked in on me, swimming through that inky blue blackness, close enough to be able to strike anytime it wants. I would be ready when it happened. That night I went home and went into the back yard. I tried to dig with my bare hands where I had buried the Tupperware container, but the dirt had hardened solid. I found a flat rock and a three-claw tool my mom had left near the fence. I went at it, breaking the soil up in clumps, then digging down into it like a rodent. It took me a while, and some busted up fingernails, before extricating the thing. My insurance was safe for now, and was going to an even safer place in the morning.

Two days later they were at the chamber of the
Arch-Lich. A couple of late night sessions pushed the
story along, and kept me grounded and sane. It blocked
out my worry. In fact, those two days were some of the
most peaceful I've ever had in my life. That night though
people started calling the store and coming in with the
tapes. I did the best I could to keep Evan out of it, but it
was shoveling against the tide. It was almost closing time
when he was finally approached by a very irate mother
who ragged his ass out and good.

At first, he had no idea what was what, but he got
wise quick since that very fucking moment a reporter
from the paper walked through the door, right up to me, a
copy of *Nightmare* in hand. I said I had no idea how this
had happened and we were going to offer full refunds to
all customers. Might have overplayed my hand when I
asked him what was on the tape.

"*You mean you don't know?*"

That's when the woman up Evan's ass starts in on
me, and I had to take it. Pulled it off well, because I just
followed Evan's lead. The reporter, some pumpkin
headed guy with a shock of white hair tells me he needs a
quote because he wants to go speak with the Chief. And
that's when I really knew the missiles were coming. A blue
winter coldness was rushing ahead of its time to burn right
through me.

Evan sat on the floor of the store after we closed.
The lights were all out. He smoked a cigarette and
crushed it out on the rug.

"What the fuck are you doing to the rug?"

"What the fuck did you do?"

"Nothing."

"Then who did that?"

"I gave him back the tapes."

"Tapes?"

"Tape whatever. Anyways, he has all the copies now. Someone got a copy and is snipping it onto our videos. We just gotta find out who rented those movies first."

"And then we will find out who duped that stuff on?"

"No doubt. Let's go get something to eat. Look Lenny is pulling up. We'll get some grub, finish Tomb and then I'll figure it all out. Okay?"

Slowly: "Okay. I want to finish this, you know."

"So do I."

He just sat there looking at me.

"You mean Tomb of Horrors, right?" I said.

Evan stood up slowly. "Better than hanging around here all alone, I guess."

Lenny drove us to Wendy's in his boxy little Audi to pick up the supplies we needed. Evan sat in the front and said nothing to me. We fish bowled the car and by the time we parked back near the store in the lot, it was hard to make out what smoke was inside the car and what was outside, pouring out of the black husk of what was my store.

Evan and I booked over to the yellow barriers the firefighters had set up, pushing through a crowd of gawkers, yelling we owned the place. No one paid us any mind. Within another twenty minutes or so, our entire store, the one we busted our nuts off for, was nothing but a hollow of burnt wood and cruelly twisted plastic, staring out from the mouth of this big brick building. One firefighter say to another, "At least we were able to contain it from spreading."

After the thing was a smoldering joke, the cops came over and were less than sympathetic. They asked us where we had been and what we were up to and who could vouch for us. We told them and they wrote it all down without much emotion. Everything unpeeled from the scene around us. Lenny went missing, or maybe he said goodbye, and Evan and I were alone on the sidewalk, inhaling these awful rust colored fumes still coming out of the blown open windows. I was hoping it would kill me. We both sat there, passing a joint until it was, like everything else, burnt to nothingness. One of us started to cry. Then it was both of us. Then it was me until I started laughing and pulling out some of my hair.

"He stole your car. He burnt down our shop, didn't he?"

"I dunno."

"I know he did this. But *why?* We did everything he asked, didn't we?"

I say nothing.

He is up and screaming: "You *fucking idiot! He knew.* No doubt the Chief knew because you were stupid enough to let him know, weren't you? And you were the one who put all those clips in those videos weren't you?"

"Why are you blaming me?"

"Because you were the only one who could have. I should have seen that right off. Maybe I should have seen a lot of things. Maybe I am a fucking idiot to trust a *piece of shit* like you! This is all your fault," pointing over like some bullshit ringmaster towards what was once ours.

I watched the orangey water wash over my sneakers. My feet should have been freezing, but weren't.

"Why then did you even *keep* a copy of that thing?"

"Security."

"Go get rid of it. Jesus, get rid of it."

"I will," standing up.

I walked past Evan without looking at him. Took my car out of the lot and scored some grub, then went back to my place. I ate and smoked and didn't give a fuck anymore. There were no lights on in the house and tomorrow morning dad would hear about the store on the news and hear the news about the Chief's tape showing up. He'd figure it all out before finishing his morning piss. It didn't matter anymore, by noon everyone in the city would know, and maybe put it all together. Even if they don't, it was all over now. I had created what I guess I ultimately wanted: mutual destruction.

Two days after the store burned down, I am on the phone in my place talking to the insurance company, a clip of the Chief's starring performance, digitized heavily, playing on the TV, when there's all this pounding on my door. Look out the window in time to see ten of them rushing through it. They flash an arrest warrant and cuff me. Shut the fuck up even though I don't know why they're busting me. They bring me downtown and I am in a cell with ink on my fingers. That's what these motherfuckers do to you.

Call Evan's uncle, but he isn't in the office. Call Evan and then Carrie, but they won't talk to me. I had no choice. You can imagine how it goes, yet a lawyer shows up within an hour. He is a real Atticus Finch, and has me brought down to the courthouse where they set my bail at $50,000. I almost shit my pants. My lawyer calls a bail bondsman down to the jail, and within an hour I am walking out of that piss hole. My dad is there to meet me outside. We get into his car and ride in silence for a bit. Then he breaks.

"This has to have something with what happened to the Chief."

I just sort of nod.

"What the hell? *Jesus.* What the hell did you do?"

The sun is in and out, but the wipers squeal away on a salt-dry windshield. He can't seem to hear the sliding screams.

"You don't even seem bothered by this, you know that? You know that Henry?"

"It's all just too much."

"You're not thinking of doing what the Chief did are you?"

"O God no. I've got enough problems as it is."

The Chief: what were you? Walking through the house one more time... The two kids still at your yellow breakfast bar, unconscious from whatever you put into their ice cream. Neither flinched when you pulled the trigger the first time and missed the youngest; your hands shaking too much. But you got it right after a quick pull from that bottle. This isn't the first time snuffing someone; not even close. They weren't even your own. And then upstairs to go look at your other handiwork. You must have really hated her. And she hated you for being a faggot in disguise. She was drowning anyways in that steady-stream-every-day fear you loved to generate. So why use that broomstick? Your hands stung after smacking her in the head with it 40 or 50 times, didn't they? You'd choke her out, let her recover, and then start all over again.

Then you give her the cruelest gift of all–hope. You let her run, terrified but mute, her larynx all but crushed; yet she ran down those stairs so she could see her children one last time. Police believe she ran to the stairs and fell, which ultimately caused her death. But we know better. You drag her right back up, and then as hard as you could, launched her head first downward. Her head made that empty melon sound when it hit the door. After a quick chuckle, we made our self a few drinks. That sort of showed the way. The way to the Avenues where you're spotted sticking your head out a cruiser window screaming at the whores, waving your gun around.

It's that hotel where we run the stings. In the distance I see the missiles coming down over red city dawn-scapes. Mushroom clouds rise and fall and shadows are painted all over the scalded landscape. They won't get me. They can't. Placing the gun to my temple. It is so cold. Trigger never been so heavy. Pull it but–no–but–White pain on my right side. Rearview mirror shows me it is just a scratch. Jesus, can't I even do this right? Maybe I am that worthless. Pick it up again with shaking hands and–just a blinding flash across my face. Blind. In the white darkness and the sirens are closing in. No more options. There is the barrel and there is the trigger–temple–pull

"First your brother, then mother, and now you. Now you... What a great job I've done."

"Dad... All I can say is I'm sorry. I'm a fuck up, but I didn't do anything this time. Please believe me. I need you to believe me."

"I really thought this time you turned things around. I guess not."

He stopped at a light and I hopped out and started walking. At the green, he drove right past me without looking my way. I was a few streets away from where my store lay full of ash and melted plastic, the fire fighters covered the window frames with these big black curtains and said it would not be safe to go inside for at least another week, due to the materials that were burnt. I had no money for a cab. Did that old walk down to the bank, went inside, got our joint safety box, and unlocked it alone in that little room. The tapes of us saying that if anything happened to us or the place were gone. The boot I had made of the original tape was gone. Only thing in that coffin was a white business envelope with the printed return address for our store on the top left corner. I took the envelope out and started turning it around and around. Tore it open by the corner, and looked inside it. Three pages of college ruled paper full on both sides with Evan's handwriting. I shoved it inside my coat, then sat there looking into the empty box. All our good times and accomplishments were now kept in there. I locked it shut.

For ten days, I stayed inside and watched the same films over and over again. I had just finished watching *Stroszek*, and was listening to Iggy Pop's *The Idiot* while doing a few things, when my phone rang. It was my lawyer asking me to come see him the next day.

"The prosecutor is going forward. It seems there is a sentiment that your unearthing of the video caused the

Chief to do what he did. However, a lot of the people do find what he did detestable. A couple of people have told me in private this was not a huge shock to them."

"He's the one who burnt down my place."

"We will talk some more about that tomorrow in my office, okay?"

"I can prove it. I can."

"Tomorrow, Henry."

When I got home the night of walking out of the car from dad, he informed me he didn't have the money to pay for my lawyer. I certainly didn't. I plead indigence and was appointed this total dickhead by the court. His name was White, and stood about six and half feet tall, yet weighed less than me. The guy was out of some small law school in upstate New York, and had been practicing for less than two years. No matter what I was most likely fucked, so what did it really matter?

I showed up the next morning with my answering machine tape. I played White the part where the Chief calls and says he is going to kill me if I fuck with him. He smiled and nodded a lot. He called the DA and set up a meeting for the next day. In that meeting with two local detectives and two other dudes, who didn't introduce themselves, they let me play my tape. Then the two strangers played a tape they brought: one starring me at the grocery store paying the guy to look the other way. Then they showed the credit card statements. They also had the note put into my auto insurance file. These two assholes turned out to be federal agents. They stood up and arrested me for several counts of federal wire fraud. Since I had been out on bail, the Feds turned me over to the locals and downtown I headed. Went through processing once more and put into a cell with one other person: the guy from the grocery store.

"You fucking cocksucker!"

He was on me in a second, whaling away like a man who can't fight, but who is gonna whip your ass anyways. He landed a bunch of good kicks and slap-punches since I just laid on the floor and let him beat on me for a while. No one came around to stop it. He injured his thumb and stopped punching me. After a while became tired of kicking me in the back, and sat down on the toilet screaming everything he could think of at me. I didn't care; I was way more fucked than him.

The next day the two of us were taken to court in a short bus along with a bunch of real undesirables. I was brought up in front of the judge, cuffed to some drunk, and had my bail revoked. I didn't hear what happened to the other jerkoff since I had dropped down the hole and into the machine, but I do know he walked out. Me they put back in the local jail which was in the basement of the police station. I would be held here until they found a bed for me in a more permanent residence. Seems the joint gets really full around the holidays.

For two days I did tried to get my lawyer to return my calls. To kill time, I watched daytime soaps through the bars and over the shoulder of the daytime guard on this tiny black and white TV. *General Hospital, Days of Our Lives, As the World Turns, The Young and the Restless.* You couldn't have any food that required utensils so it was baloney sandwiches and chips with warm tap water. That was if you could eat over the stink of unwashed men. Drunks would come and go all hours of the day, some would puke everywhere, others would just dry heave or make cave art with their shit sprays. I had my own corner of a cell with four bunks, and didn't make eye contact with anyone.

I would watch the news, which was still full of stories about the Chief and what he did. There was also plenty of talk about me and the arson case and now it was out they had me for wire fraud. Evan and Carrie were not speaking to the press, even though for a few days after my arrest, the news trucks camped out in front of their place. I was made to look like some psycho worse than the Chief. Film was played of the cops harassing me in front of the Coldwell house. It was mentioned I was kicked out of college for drugs. Combining the Chief and I into one mega-story, a one-in-the-same monster, ratings must have been amazing. My lawyer was constantly on the screen stating I had nothing to do with the Chief's rampage or the fire at my store. Right then I knew he would rather get his face out there, then call me or try to get me out of the shit.

Only once did that fraud visit me in the jail. Cameras must not have been around him that day. This got me out of my cell and into a closet of a room with one lightbulb above. After some niceties, we got down on it.

"I didn't burn my store down, and they can't prove that I did."

"There are some things here, Henry, that look bad. They have some videos with you in them."

"So what?"

"I got word they are about to be made public. This is not going to help."

"O Christ."

"And your auto insurance company, the one that also insures your store... Well they released to the police and Feds and me all their notes about starting a fraud investigation on you. And these notes state you tried to bribe an adjuster to lie about how your car was damaged."

"That's a lie. It's bullshit!"

"I am not so sure how admissible it would be, but it might be, and that would be bad. I will try and say it is nothing but hearsay and speculation."

"Yeah. Do anything."

"Then there are the Federal charges which are more concrete and they also have the guy at the counter turned and ready to testify against you."

"What if I testify against him in his case?"

"They don't care about him, Henry. They're not pressing charges and they're promising him immunity. You're a big name out there right now."

"Jesus Christ. I mean, what does this all mean?"

"There is a lot of bad feeling out there on you. It's not like you did terrible things at all, but the press has made you look like a monster. One TV station must have gotten the cease and desist letters you were sent and that's been all over the news. They're making you look like a real criminal. I'm doing my best, but I've also got thirteen other cases to handle. Plus, these videos with the prostitute."

Stood there in silence looking at my socks over my shower sandals. Wasn't sure if I was going to shit or faint, but I knew I wanted out of that room.

"What's going to happen to me?"

"Perhaps the Commonwealth will agree to let you plead to something, and then we plead to something on the Federal level, then maybe you could do your time in a Club Fed."

"I'm gonna do time? For fucking what?"

"Well the state is going to go to trial with an arson case against you. And then certainly the Feds are going to go after you for wire fraud. I think-"

"-No fucking time."

"-Listen to me. If you plead and let me work this out, you could be back out in eighteen months. Sit in the Club Fed and meet some rich people and get some connections and work out. All white. Don't worry. You go to Walpole, we you all know what can happen to you there. You wouldn't make it Henry. And if you did what you would have to do-"

"-Okay, okay, okay. Do your absolute best to keep me out of prison, okay?"

"I'll do everything I can for you."

Six days before Christmas the DA, a federal agent and my lawyer all met with me at the courthouse where I signed a new agreement. I would agree to plead guilty to the Commonwealth for *wanton or reckless destruction or injury by fire*, pay $500 and take a ten-year probation deal. I would then be taken over to Federal Court in Worcester, where I will plead guilty to one count of federal wire fraud, and spend up to sixty months at a minimum-security prison. If they forced me to go to trial on Arson One, and I went down on it, I'd be looking at easily a solid ten years in Walpole. Fuck that, I could never survive there. The bitch was that I had to plead to reckless destruction before the Feds would cut me the deal. Everyone knew that they could no doubt put me away on wire fraud, since I was stupid enough to be filmed. When I turned to the clerk after he mentioned Ian, the camera caught me perfectly. So much for movies where the State and Fed undercut each other.

With my back to the wall, I signed the thing, and on Christmas Eve day, I was transferred to the Worcester County House of Detention where I was kept in a cell alone waiting for my TB test to come back. The air conditioner was on constantly, and I stayed under this cheap cotton blanket while huddled on this concrete slab. Three days later they shipped me out to a Federal Pen in upstate New York. I was kept in iso for 48 hours there until all my med tests came back, then I was housed with Caucasian coke dealers and serious users, crooked accountants, shiftless CEOs, a few other disgraced businessmen. There were some Italians who kept to themselves during yard time, and lived in another part of the complex. About eighty percent of the place was white, and the races never mixed except for business. I was assigned a top bunk in a dirty gray basketball gymnasium with about 200 bunkbeds packed in tightly. I slept a lot during the day when I could, then stayed up all night playing movies in my head. Maybe a lot of these people were respectable outside, but in here they turned feral. You could hear the cock suckers and ass fuckers, the seething wanderers looking for a warm hole. One guy was such a homo that he somehow got estrogen injections while inside. At all times, I carried two bars of soap in a sock, hidden down the back of my sweats.

I kept to myself as much as possible. The only thing I did that was social, and it was only to earn good time credit, was teach a class on film to some of the more intelligent inmates. I caught some shit for showing *A*

Clockwork Orange, but only because of the nudity, not its message. I told them I was going to show it, and the CO said "sure, sure." Totally their fault. That was really the only thing I looked forward to my whole time there. I even missed the Super Bowl. The Friday before the game I received a letter from the insurance company saying that because I had plead to wanton and reckless of my own property, they were not going to pay out on the $50,000 policy we had taken out. Once I read that I had a little meltdown and started throwing all the shit from my footlocker all over the place, yelling, screaming, swinging away with my sock sap. I caught one on the guards on the top of the head, not very hard, but they don't care. Three of them slammed me onto the concrete floor, roughed me up good and chucked me into iso.

It became fascinating having no concept of what time it was; even having no use for such a concept is interesting. I free floated, coming to a lot of realizations about myself in that awful little cell; most of them not very comforting. Kept a pillow or this washcloth I'd wet over my eyes most of the time. My eyes adjusted and could see through that darkness. Really worked on building something inside in my heart. Tried to change, but the deeper I got into myself, the more I knew I never could. For some reason, I am rotten. That's all there is really. I asked to stay in iso the rest of my time, but they said no. While I was in there my mom, of all people, had put $30 in my book. She must have been feeling super guilty. One of the advantages of an overcrowded prison is that if you are not in for drug charges, most likely they aren't going to test you. I went right to the dope man and bought six joints with my thirty clams. I smoked them slowly over about a week. That helped me stay in check.

Wrote to my dad every week, and for the first few months, nothing. Then he did write me, just talking about work mostly. I knew he hated me. I did everything I could not to think of it. I wrote him to hurt myself. No doubt the wrong kid died in my family. After a while we stopped communicating and I took to staring at the ceiling. It made me feel even worse, but I wanted to feel as badly as I possibly could. It is what I deserved for putting him through this. For a while I wanted to stay locked up forever, because I knew life would never be as good as it had been. And then there were all the ghosts waiting for me upon my return.

One day while these thunderstorms were going on and we had no yard time, I tried writing Evan. Don't know why. I went all the way back and thought about all the amazing times we had had together. Those marathon D&D games, driving late at night on the highways and backroads signing to anything but Rush, and opening the place with him. He was the guy I went to when my mom flaked. But we did it, and for a while it was Nirvana. But Nirvana never lasts. He could have been a better friend though and believed me. The shit looked bad, but he still could have heard me out. I signed the thing, sincerely Henry, then tore it up.

If Evan wanted to be a man he could contact me, and then I would tell him everything. I wanted to tell him everything, to him *and* Carrie. I would tell them what I could, because I didn't know why I did some of what I did. Eventually, I did hear from both: through letters from their family lawyers. They were demanding for Evan

$50,000: $25,000 for his lost share of the insurance, another half for lost potential income. They wanted $15,000 for Carrie for the tanning bed and potential loss of revenue. I flushed both letters down a toilet, along with the one from the safety deposit box that I never bothered to read.

A heap of demands came my way, all with the threats of court. They knew I had no way to pay; this was pure revenge for things I hadn't even done to them. Evan was my best friend, I never wanted him caught up in this. Her either. But there was just something that was in my head, and no matter what, I couldn't help myself. It's a pretty helpless feeling when you don't want to think about something, but o shit here it comes like a motherfucking freight train. You put up a brick wall. The engine smashes head first into it. It's a crash so severe that you don't have to ask if there are any survivors.

Court dates were set, but I didn't even know when or where they were. I could have gotten a day out of the pen, but instead stayed on my bed. I was found guilty in absentia, and they were awarded what they asked, plus court costs and legal fees. Soon letters started coming about that too, but I didn't even bother to open them. What were they going to do, lock me up?

I caught my first break in a long time on the Fourth of July. Seems this huge biker war came to a head in one of the Dakotas and there were hundreds of arrests. They wanted to spread the dudes all over the place to keep their numbers low in any one facility, so they needed space. And since almost all of them had outstanding warrants or were on probation, back to the Fed most of them were sent. This caused overcrowding and violence to go way up, and the higher ups here were not pleased. Since they couldn't let the bikers go, the next thing we knew, they were letting all the nonviolent people out. October 1, out the door I walk, doing a little under a year in the pen.

Took a bus back to the nearest town, and then another back to Massachusetts. I had permission to leave New York, with orders to meet my PO within 48 hours and get a job ASAP. I arrived in town at 11 p.m., and walked for almost an hour to get back home. I took my keys to prison with me, and stored them in the lock box at intake. I snuck up the back stairs and the locks were still the same. My father had cleaned out the whole place. Only my bed and dresser remained. I put my bindle on the floor and used it as a pillow.

Dad driving out for work woke me up. I was flat on my back and hungry as hell. My house key still worked so I made myself a baloney and Wonder Bread sandwich and left not a crumb. I was dying for caffeine since it was hard to come by in the can. There was no soda in the house, so I made a big, harsh cup of Sanka in the microwave and downed it quickly. I cleaned the cup, put it back where I found it, then went back to the apartment and straightened up there. I had a few changes of clothing in my bag, and put on a gray sweatshirt and some white jeans.

I locked everything up and went down to my old car. Took the "for-sale" sign that was sitting behind a new windshield and put it on the front passenger's seat. Got in and turned it over with a little bit of finesse. My insurance had expired, but I wasn't going to be gone long. The first thing I did was go get some McNuggets and a huge Coke.

There will never be anything more delicious and sweet as that first bite and sip. I had refrained from the canteen the best I could in jail, which is why I had fifty bucks left in my pockets after the bus ride home. Evan and I used to smoke that over a weekend.

I was now on parole and would be drug tested, so I went around and got a bottle of cheap vodka. Would have killed for maybe some nice wine coolers, but this shit was way cheaper. Pulled into the parking lot across from my old store. Sat there and watched the construction underway. It was being converted to one of the new chain record stores. Drank about a fifth of the bottle, got a small drunk on and cried for a good half an hour. This was still prison, so I said fuck it, found a phone booth and after a couple of calls found a hookup. Drove down to the grocery store where I scored the cash not so long ago, and met the dealer in the parking lot. I bought some rolling papers in a drug store in the same strip, rolled a tight one, then smoked it like a butt while driving.

It was passing the roach stage when I arrived in front of Evan's house. Parked across the street under a big white tree with no leaves. This place has a perfectly manicured lawn, and two lawn jockeys on each side of the driveway's entrance. No matter what happens to Evan, he will be taken care of; at least I have that. It really is reason I didn't kill myself right in front of his house. Sat there smoking a smaller joint and sipping the shitty booze. There wasn't anything that could get me wasted enough to ring that doorbell. Drove back to my old apartment, returning before my dad, put the sign back in the car window, then hid in my old place. It was cold as hell up there with no power. I watched dad come home, walk into his empty house with his head down, and melt into the darkness.

I sat on the floor and fucking bawled my eyes out. Bawled and bawled until dad unlocked the door and came in. He sat down next to me and for the first time in my life, I saw him cry. We didn't hug or touch, or any gay shit like that, but we cried together and let some of that bullshit go. Then we got straight with each other; It took until past the sun coming up.

We both agreed that I should leave town, because people were blaming me for the Chief going nuts, and for burning my place down. The worst goddamn thing I ever did was trust that lawyer and take that deal. I should have fought this thing with everything I had. Dad knew I was damned here, and this place held nothing for me now. He never asked me the real story, and I am glad, because I doubt he really wants to know.

We also agreed I should call Evan and just let him take it all out on me. It was the right thing to do. That night I plugged a phone into a jack in my old room and called the house. I tried to disguise my voice a bit when some man answered. He asked who I was and I gave the name Ian Curtis. I could hear the phone being set down, and silence. Then there were some murmurs and then: "Hello?" with an edge.

"Is Evan there, please?"

"You know what *fuck you*, you asshole. You owe me thousands of dollars, and you owe Evan a lot more. You owe Evan his life back."

"Is he there?"

"*No.*"

"When will he be in?"

"Look Henry, don't call back. He doesn't want to hear from you."

"I just want to talk to him."

"Even if he did want to scream at your sorry ass for a few months, he can't. He doesn't live here right now."

"Where is he?"

"Boston."

"You know his number?"

"He doesn't want to *hear from you*! Trust me. What don't you just go find a fucking place to go die."

"Whatever."

"Don't call back Henry. The damage is done."

She hung up and eventually I did too. Took out my notebook from prison, sat on my bed, and wrote a long letter to Evan and another to Carrie. I told them the truth the best I could figure it, knowing they would hate me forever. I put them into a big envelope, and addressed it to their main house. My dad brought it to the post office for me the next morning.

My P.O. granted me permission to move out of state and go live with my mother. Since I was a federal case, it was a bit easier to switch offices and officers. The day after Thanksgiving, after one of the best days we ever had together, I accepted $200 and a firm handshake from dad. I headed out in my unregistered, uninspected car. All I had to do was get out of state and the police wouldn't harass me for my sticker. I didn't look back as I pulled down the street. Drove the seven hours, stopping only twice, and got to my mother's new place while it was still light out. She and Cris had cleared out a nice room for me. I put what few things I had in there, then sat on the bed.

That Monday I went downtown and met with my new P.O. She gave me some shit for not having a job when I was home, but I promised her I would get one right away. And because it was this or back to the can, I found work. One of those video chain stores was opening here, so I went out and was interviewed by some 40-year-old dumbass named Mister Sausage or something that didn't know Herschel Gordon Lewis from Kenneth Anger. Blew him away so much the fuck *had* to hire me. My first hour working there I saw this was nothing but another soulless place where all you get out of it is a few sheckles and a lot less time for real living. You can't get high on parole, but you can get the booze out of your system before they test you.

I was pretty much drunk all the time; buzzed at work, passed out at home. In February, I got off parole and had already cultivated a weed connection at the store. She came through for me right away and I got high in my mom's garage, staring at a Quaker State can for over an hour. Cris was a heavy Merit smoker, so it covered up the stink for me. One night we even smoked up together. This was really doing nothing but numbing me out. My mom charged me no rent out of sheer guilt, and so all my cash went to food, films and dope.

But that job was killing me. Started thinking I might have been happier when I was back in prison, where at least I could see my bars. Here the place was an open gulag. You had to get permission to take a piss and they really looked down on taking a shit during non-break time. Then there were rumors that drug testing was going

to become a companywide policy. This was really
something that I could not have. I usually walked to the
place, since it was only about a mile away, and one day in
late March I was so dreading dealing with all these film
philistines and bullshit company policies that I called in a
bomb threat from a payphone right near the place. I
showed up ten minutes later, and in the parking lot Mister
Sausage was having a meltdown.

"Did you take the call?" I said.

"Yes."

Sirens were becoming clearer.

"What did the guy sound like?"

"Just like Freddy Kruger."

"Weird."

He sent me home, saying he didn't want to pay
me for standing around all day in his parking lot. Like the
money comes right out of his pocket or something and
the whole fucking lot was owned by him. Asshole. He's
the biggest fool I've ever met, not even able to see his own
truth. When I got home there were several letters from
lawyers and the state department of revenue. Because I
never showed up for the civil trials or paid a cent, a judge
was allowing them to now garnish my pay. By the time I
paid taxes *and* that, I'd barely make anything. I went to
the library and did some looking into my situation. Things
became much clearer, and right away I knew what to do
to piss off these mighty and moneyed motherfuckers
trying to run my life.

Another day at the office

     Two days ago at work I was up on a ladder screwing in a fluorescent light tube. As soon as no one was looking I flung myself off it and splatted on the floor. Didn't land it quite right, and crunched my knee which hurt like a fucker. Laid still as I could, crying out in pain loudly. My mother's doctor up here, the one Cris got her, the one they all call Pills Renzo, ruled me out for at least 6 months with a damaged ligament. I immediately called the revenue department and let them know what had happened. They let me know that once I was off workman's comp that I would have my pay garnished once again, and interest could be compiling if I did not begin payback quickly. I thanked them for the information.

I lay on the bed sort of looking down at myself for a moment. This moment is far too long. I look tired and old and no good to anyone, least of all myself. When I return my mind is quite clear. I've fought too hard and too long for this to continue. I have done my time and now I want to be free again. Some guys in the pen liked it there because they only had to worry about protecting their ass and nothing else. Some guys didn't even have to worry about that. Not me, I hated every fucking, self-torturing second of it. I was cool with people, especially dealers, but I made no friends there, or even tried. The day I got off that bus and jumped out in front of this check cashing place, something resembling happiness raced through me; the chance to be truly free once more.

But that time is so many years away that once I do reach it, I will be so spent and conditioned by this machine, what will be left of my soul? That is the worst burden to bear; even if I make it again, it will never be the same, and it will come at such a huge price. To wait for that day is an almost madness inducing thought; the years to come once again in the darkness. Even if my debts are forgiven, so what? It draws that day almost no closer. I must pay the machine again, but I don't have it in me to do it even one more day. There will be a time when I will be forced to make decisions about this, but that isn't today.

Walk with my crutches into the hall making sure no one has stopped by the house. My leg brace is black and the metal hinges dig into me if I move around too much. The place is empty and the wind is blowing like crazy against the windows. I take the cord out of the wall, bring it to my room, and plug it in here. Set up all my things, then light up some peppermint incense. I work my way down onto this this big blue bean bag I bought at Caldors, and set the phone to the side. This hot plate Cris gave me is heating up water for my Ramen Noodles. I had a little glass pipe I picked up at a smoke shop on my walk home one day, which is full of some okay stuff. Nothing like the olden days though. I do what I do. I pick up the phone and set it on my lap. Everything is okay now. It won't be in a few hours, but it is at this moment. Right now, my biggest problem is figuring out how to kill my time.

www.ingramcontent.com/pod-product-compliance
Lightning Source LLC
Chambersburg PA
CBHW071939170626
46813CB00005B/1791